AVENGED INNOCENCE

Elle Iverson

This book is a work of fiction.
Names, characters, places, and incidents either are products of the author's imagination or are used fictitiously.
Any resemblance to actual events or locales, or persons, living or dead, is entirely coincidental.

Copyright © 2019 by Stacey Spangler

All rights reserved.
Including the right to reproduce this book or portions thereof in any form whatsoever.

ISBN: 9781794010499

This book is dedicated to everyone else who is also just a little off… and to all the other people who also have quirks and strange obsessions.

We make this world interesting.

PROLOGUE

A dozen eight-year-olds pinball their way through an inflatable bounce house that is set up on the spacious front yard of a classic Victorian-style home at the end of a quiet cul-de-sac.

The sun is shining and the slight breeze cools off the warm summer afternoon. The delighted squeals of the children fill the air of the Minneapolis suburb.

Pink and silver balloons decorate the mailbox and cars line the circle driveway. The parents are dispersed on the lush green lawn, chitchatting as they watch the little ones playing games and frolicking through the inflatables. The moms discuss the upcoming neighborhood garage sale while the dads banter over baseball starting line-ups.

The birthday girl is adorned in a flowing pink gown with sequence stitched across the top and a tiara completing her outfit. She comes bounding toward her mother. The sun reflecting off the shimmering dress, surrounding her in an array of sparkles.

The girl appears to be glowing as she leaps into her mother's outstretched arms. The little girl is the spitting image of her runway-ready mother. A pint-size version of the stunning beauty with flaxen locks, large green eyes, and sun-kissed skin. Her blonde ringlets bounce up and down as the little girl excitedly asks about the cake, is it time yet?

Her mother smiles, kisses her gently on the cheek and whispers, "Almost." Then she sets her down and lovingly shoos her away. Disappointed, but knowing she shouldn't pout, the little girl slowly slinks back towards her friends and the large purple blow-up castle.

Suddenly a siren cuts through the air, silencing the chatter and the giggles. Everyone turns toward the sound as a firetruck rounds the corner at the end of the street.

Lights on.

Siren blaring.

Horn honking.

The little girl's eyes fill with tears as she rushes toward the commotion. Her mother grabs her by the shoulders and is able to keep her still until the truck comes to a complete stop.

As soon as the mother loosens her grip, the little girl runs at full speed (curls bouncing, dress sparkling) and throws herself at the fireman who is stepping onto the curb.

The handsome man bends down, scoops up the little girl, and nuzzles his face into her soft hair. Then he pulls a large pink teddy bear from behind his back and nestles it into her side.

"Happy Birthday, Princess. I wouldn't have missed this for the world." He effortlessly holds the little girl with one arm while he wraps the other around the waist of her mother. He pulls the blonde beauty close to him and kisses her passionately; either oblivious to the crowd watching or indifferent to them.

Two young boys run from the group of children.
"Daddy!" They exclaim, as excited as their sister about the surprise. The five-year-old wraps himself around one of the fireman's legs. The eleven-year-old grins and gives his dad a high-five before throwing his arms around the birthday girl and their mom.

Smiles radiate.
The family embraces.
Joy is etched on their faces.
Happiness fills their hearts.
The picture perfect day is complete.

It would be their last.

CHAPTER 1

I wake to the smell of garbage burning my nostrils. I instinctively pull my shirt over my face to block the stench. When I move my other arm over my head (to shield my eyes from the blinding rays of the rising sun) I smash my fist into the dumpster beside me.

That explains the stench.

I sit up and roll my neck, my face twisting into a grimace as the tight muscles protest in pain. I feel much older than my nineteen years.

My backpack, which doubles as my pillow, isn't exactly a feathery-down, Tempur-Pedic cloud like you might see on a TV commercial. And instead of greeting the day with a smile and a cup of Folgers, I'm starting off with a kinked neck next to a pile of, what we'll pretend is, spilled chowder.

I yawn and readjust my stretch to avoid the dumpster. I keep my eyes closed for another couple minutes to enjoy the soundtrack of the city. Horns honking, distant chatter, and dishes clanging. I get a pleasant whiff of coffee as it momentarily masks the garbage stink.

I hear the powerful sound of a waste management truck downshifting. The tune of the garbage man means it's about seven a.m.

One benefit of living on the street is the variety of alarm clocks. I have time for one final stretch and then I need to get moving.

Today is a big day.

I interlock my fingers and reach my hands above my head, letting my chin rest near my chest, extending my neck.

A conventional stretch for another nonconventional day.

My stomach growls.

I would kill for a big breakfast right about now. But unless I want to feast on the rotten eggs and discarded bacon fat from the small diner on the other side of this dumpster, it looks like I'll settle for an off-brand granola bar yet again. It might not be a gourmet spread but I am looking forward to enjoying it on my walk this morning. It'll be the perfect snack once I get moving. I grab the last one from the front zipper of my bag (it's chocolate chip, my favorite) and slip it in the back pants pocket of my jeans.

I know I smell like the heap of trash I spent the night next to, and even though I'm used to it, I am really looking forward to freshening up.

Which happens to be the first thing on today's agenda.

I brush off the flecks of who-knows-what from my shirt and stand to stretch my legs.

I fold up the remaining half of my favorite blanket, gently handling the satin material, and carefully place it into its designated pocket of my very mobile home.

Everything I own is within arm's length at all times.

Most transients have some sort of vessel to store their belongings: Shopping carts, suitcases, and plastic bags are a few of the favorites. But the most common, and my personal preference, is a backpack.

I've cleverly nicknamed mine Pac.

Pac isn't any run-of-the-mill back-to-school special. No, it is top-of-the-line military grade Army pack.

Avenged Innocence

It was my daddy's. He was a lieutenant in the Army before he retired and became a fireman.

Now his Pac holds my life.

Not only is it my most valuable possession, it's my only one.

When I say it holds my life, I'm not being dramatic. It literally contains my whole world.

It has for the past four years.

Ever since I left Minnesota.

Ever since I became homeless.

Ever since I became Christina.

CHAPTER 2

I slip Pac over my shoulders and head out of the alley toward the interstate. I peer between the buildings as I walk by, trying to take in the view of the skyline. I've been tucked into this corner of the city for about a month, but this sight still takes my breath away.

The giant glass buildings loom over the spider web-looking contraption of concrete roads that lay out underneath. It's an engineering marvel.

I smile and flip my wrist in a friendly wave as I pass a trio of familiar faces. I'm as close to this group as I have been to anyone in years, and I still don't know them very well. Everyone has a story and a real name; but we don't get into those.

The three guys who are leaning against the rundown storefront window are the core of my latest group.

There's SC. He looks like an emaciated Santa Clause. I'm willing to bet that's what SC stands for, though I've never asked.

Next to him, staring blankly up and to the left, is Spaz. He's mindlessly flicking his right ear. He's a little off. I don't know exactly what's wrong with him (he probably doesn't either) but I

Avenged Innocence

heard he self-medicates by experimenting with different drugs. He's weird but harmless.

Next to Spaz (meeting my gaze but not returning the smile) is Lee. Few people make me as nervous as Lee does. With his wild beard, beady eyes, and sleeves of tattoos, he reminds me of an angry biker. His imposing size and menacing glare have had me on edge since I ventured into this part of town.

Even though I don't know them very well, they have their own security network and they have extended it to include me. That's the reason I was actually able to sleep by the dumpster. We take turns playing lookout. You never know what might happen… but it helps to have the strength in numbers.

I never stay in one place very long. Even so, I've been in this city since I was fifteen and I haven't even come close to covering it all. And now I'm moving on again. I won't be returning this way, but I don't think it's necessary to say goodbye. That's one of the perks of being a transient. No real relationships but no long farewells either.

At the end of the block, tucked behind a streetlight, I see a brown scratchy wool blanket.

Neeter. Neeter reminds me of the quintessential Mexican *Abuela*. Age is hard to judge out here, but her leathery skin and gray hair suggest that she's lived more than a few decades.

I lean over and gently tap the top of the blanket. The brief touch makes my palm itch. How does she sleep in this? I see the brown sackcloth stir and two fingers pull down a corner to reveal her kind face.

"Good morning Neeter."

She offers a sleepy smile in reply.

"How are you today?" I speak slowly, briefly pausing between each word. She speaks English, but not well.

"Hambre." *Hungry.*

I think of the last granola bar in my back pocket.

My mouth waters.

My stomach growls again.

But my hand reaches into my pocket instinctively, grabs the bar, and hands it to the elderly woman.

Elle Iverson

"Gracias." She mutters as my last scrap of food disappears into her scratchy cocoon.

"You're welcome, Neeter."

I will miss her.

She has been kind and welcoming. I wish I could do more for her. But I'm lacking the means and the time.

Today is a big day.

Today is meeting day.

I pick up the pace and head towards the truck stop a couple miles down the road. I could hitchhike (and sometimes I do) but I don't like to run the risk when I don't have to. I have plenty of time and it's a gorgeous morning, so I'll just enjoy the walk.

It's already about seventy-five degrees. Not bad for Dallas in August.

The traffic is always heavy this time of day. The usual breakneck speed of cars flying by is reduced to a leisurely crawl which makes it possible for me to play 'Guess Who's Driving'. That's a game I invented where I make up the backstory of the driver and try to figure out where they're going and what they've been through. It helps to pass the time and it keeps my mind sharp. I know the stalled lanes frustrate the commuters but it gives me a chance to actually see the drivers. Most of them look the same. Businessmen in gas-conscious, mid-size cars. Good guys just heading to work. Every once in a while I'll see a unique getup and those stories are especially fun to imagine.

Take this guy for example, in a Volkswagen van that is riddled with stickers. He is obviously blitzed out of his mind. He has the scraggly beard, zoned expression, and even a tie-dye shirt. All he's missing is a pair of small, round sunglasses and an exaggerated puff of smoke drifting out of the window. I decide he's heading for a job interview at a prestigious law firm.

He goes by 'Ziggy' and he's "totally ready to do law and stuff, Dude.". Oh, to be a fly on the wall for that discussion…

Then there's this poor mom in a minivan. I count three kids in the back. Two are screaming and the third is expertly taking off

Avenged Innocence

his shoes and socks and tossing them next to his car seat. Mom is staring straight ahead and I can almost see her counting to ten. And back down. Then to ten again.

To her credit, she doesn't lose it. She definitely deserves that giant vat of coffee she's sipping on.

Good job, Mom. I'm guessing she's running late for yoga. She doesn't really like yoga but the studio offers free childcare so she goes every week.

A few cars behind her is a small, blue, two-door being driven by a pretty redhead who appears to be in her early twenties, just a few years older than me. She's talking on a cell phone. Smiling and laughing.

I know better than to judge on first impressions, but if I had to guess, I would say she's happy. Probably not care-free (no one really has that luxury) but happy. She's headed to a job she enjoys but that isn't her career. She's still finding herself. Maybe she has a boyfriend. She definitely has a best friend. Maybe even a couple really good friends, too. She's close to her mom. Still daddy's little girl. Maybe that's who is on the phone.

I feel a tinge of jealousy creep in so I shift my focus to the next car. An older lady who is hunched over the steering wheel and looks like she's sitting on a phone book, squinting to see the car in front her.

That's not safe.

My mind drifts back to the happy-looking redhead. I wonder, if circumstances had been different, could I have ever led a normal life?

I'm not envious of her or the minivan mom. I'm glad there are people who can simply live their lives. It is part of the reason I do what I do. So people can enjoy their mornings and laugh with their friends. So stressed out moms can drink their coffee in chaos. So Volkswagen guy can get lit before breakfast.

I do what I do so others can remain oblivious.

My brokenness helps keep society whole.

My purpose is to use my tragedy to protect the innocent.

CHAPTER 3

The traffic picks up as I near the truck stop.

It's an older location, just off the interstate. There's a large gravel parking lot in the back, a bay of diesel pumps for trucks, and a separate bay of gas pumps for cars.

There are quite a few rigs coming and going.

I slip in the side door, doing my best to remain unseen. They don't much care for drifters at places like this… or anywhere, really. As a general rule we're looked on as more of an infestation of pests rather than humans who need help. The type of help that is needed differs with each individual but in my experience; if someone is living on the street then they need help in one form or another.

I walk quickly to the restroom. I open the door and almost run into Elizabeth Taylor.

Ok, it's not really her but they could be twins. Big black hair, dark red lipstick, and flashy jewelry. She is wearing a shimmering silver pantsuit and is surrounded by a mist of an expensive-smelling perfume. She is carrying an oversized red supple-leather purse that she clutches to her chest when she sees me.

She glares at me with disdain for having the nerve to enter this public restroom. I step to the side and hold the door open for her. She walks by with an audible 'huff' as she leaves.

Well, Good Morning to you, too.

Avenged Innocence

I let the door close and I walk to the counter where I slide Pac off my back.

I glance up and catch a glimpse of my reflection in the mirror.

Is that really my reflection?

I'm disappointed to see that I look as gross as I feel.

No wonder judgement was radiating off of the glamourous grandma. The phrase dirty blonde may never have been so accurate as right now.

I have my work cut out for me today.

My shoulder-length, golden hair is streaked with highlights from the sun and lowlights from, what appears to be…motor oil?

My eyes (which my mama used to say looked like magical emeralds) are unnoticeable thanks to the smudges of dirt riddling my face and the fact that the sockets are sunken in so low I look like a skeleton donning a blondish wig.

To complete the ambiance, my skin has a nice ashen hue to it.

Holy Moly.

How long has it been since I showered? Lemme think…

I guess it's probably been about ten days. Last week's meeting was cancelled so it would have been the one before that, when he ended up being a no-show. But I had made myself presentable.

I make a mental note to shower every week.

Maybe even twice a week.

But that's not always easy. A lot of fuel stations have updated to electronic showers where you have to scan a card or have a rewards membership to use the facilities. This is the only one I know of that's still outdated enough to have a small showering section next to the back bathrooms. That's one reason it is my favorite.

I grab Pac and a small stack of paper towels sitting on the counter. When I do, I notice a red supple-leather coin purse that had fallen behind them. I pick it up and unhook the silver clasp. A large roll of cash is shoved in so tightly that some of it spills out immediately. Hundred dollar bills. There are a few twenties, but mostly hundreds.

I take a deep breath then force out a loud sigh. Dang it.

I toss Pac back over my shoulder and rush out of the bathroom. I scan the busy truck stop and easily spot the black hair and silver pantsuit walking out the front door. Red purse hanging at her side.

I catch up with her just as she's unlocking her convertible. The color of the purse matches the car; the leather of the purse matches the interior. Very nice.

"Excuse me, Ma'am?"

She spins around with a hateful expression but offers no words.

"I think you dropped this in the restroom."

She studies the small bag in my outstretched hand. She eyes me suspiciously before grabbing it and securing it in her purse; which she continues to grip as she gets in, locks the car, starts the engine, and backs away.

No need to thank me or offer any monetary compensation for my good deed. Your happiness is reward enough.

I walk back through the truck stop, into the empty bathroom, grab the stack of paper towels and turn to the mirror. I look at my pitiful reflection one more time and say, "Good job. That was the right thing to do."

Then I leave the blonde skeleton behind and go to the showers. There are tables and lockers available for occupants to leave their belongings while they wash up, but Pac is never out of my sight. Ever. So I set it in the corner of the stall and take out my shower kit. It's a gallon-sized baggie that contains shampoo, conditioner, soap, shaving cream, and a razor.

I turn the nozzle on and give it a minute to warm up. While it does, I carefully take off my clothes, fold them into another gallon-sized baggie, and tuck them into their designated pocket.

By now the steam from the water is rising around me and I step under the faucet. I can feel the hot rivers running down my body, eroding away the dirt and grime. I turn so my face is directly under the stream and breathe in deeply. Drinking in the

Avenged Innocence

humid air around the water. I feel my body relax as the current cascades around me. This is my happy place.

I take time lathering my hair and soaping up my body.

I enjoy the cleansing. I close my eyes and feel the nasty build-up that naturally occurs from living in the city (the smog, the smells, the smoke) being washed away.

Today I go through the complete routine; shaving my legs, doubly rinsing my hair, the whole shebang.

I finally shut off the water.

One extravagance I can't afford is a towel, hence the stack of paper towels. Times like this (cold, wet, and shivering) when I'm wringing out my hair and shaking my arms to drip dry, I usually consider getting one. But the reality is that Pac is already too full. There's no room.

After I've done my initial dog-like method of drying off, I grab a couple of the sandpaperish towels and pat the rest of my body dry. Then I grab another gallon baggie. This one contains my meeting outfit: a black sports bra, clean underwear, a black tank top, thigh-length jean shorts, a pair of black and white converse, and sunglasses.

I have three outfits. Meeting day, homeless, and extra. They're all pretty basic. I rotate them out occasionally, but there's only room to fit three.

I get dressed quickly and I bring Pac back to the counter. I take out another baggie. This one has a toothbrush, toothpaste, deodorant, a comb, and a few hair ties.

I run the comb through my hair (which is back to my natural dishwater blonde) and then I brush my teeth. Even after all this time, that's really my crutch. The one thing I can't let go to let this city truly claim me. I'll wear the stinky clothes. I'll rock the dirty, oily hair. I'll even let the layer of grime cover my skin. But I can't neglect my teeth. They are perfectly white, still straight, and totally healthy. (As far as I know.)

I pull my freshly-washed, lavender-scented hair into a side-braid that falls just below my collarbone.

Elle Iverson

Viola. The transformation from homeless to high-schooler is complete.

Oh, one more thing… I reach to the bottom of Pac, to the very bottom, unzip the hidden compartment and bring out my phone. I turn it on and I'm happy to see it still has 80% battery. I never have it out when I'm on the street. It's a red flag. It would practically shout that I don't belong. I guess this is another non-conforming point. But it is necessary because now it would be suspicious if I didn't have some sort of device.

One last scan in the mirror and I can't help but smile at this reflection… and the reminders of my past life it brings. Looking at me now one would think that my biggest worries were who was going to ask me to prom and whether or not I was gonna make cheer squad.

A quick image of my one and only experience at a dance flashes through my mind

I vividly remember my black gown and high heels.

And Levi. And his tux. And his smile.

That was the night that confirmed what I had expected.

The night I knew I was different.

The night I knew I was damaged.

Looking in the mirror now, there is no visible indication of the darkness that blots my soul. No outward signs of the magnitude of tragic events I ran away from.

No tell-tale clues that four years ago, at fifteen-years-old, I ran away from a near-ideal life to voluntarily assume the role of vagabond.

Well, voluntarily may be a stretch.

I had to.

I had to leave.

I didn't have a choice.

I had to do it to protect my family.

I throw Pac over my shoulder and head out of the showers.

Showtime.

CHAPTER 4

I walk from the solitude of the bathroom to the crowded central part of the truck stop. I hang back by the soda cooler for just a minute. Watching the hustle and bustle and listening to the truckers. This milling area is fairly large but fills up quickly. A few women make their way past me to the showers and a few guys make a beeline for the men's restroom. There are another dozen or so people lingering around the snack area.

It doesn't take long for me to find my mark. He looks to be about forty-years-old, big beard, trucker's belly, and a couple inches shorter than me. He's been quiet but has politely nodded a greeting to everyone who has passed. He threw away his empty sugar packets after dumping the contents into his coffee cup, and he is waiting calmly (without fidgeting) while another gentleman tries to figure out how to balance three slices of greasy pizza on top of a trough of coke.

Patient, respectful, and not in too big of a hurry.

My type of guy.

The campus where my meeting is set to happen is about ten miles away and I need a ride. I walk towards the trucker, blinking my eyes rapidly to produce a base of tears.

"Excuse me, Sir?" He turns to me and I continue, "I'm so sorry to bother you. My school bus just left without me and I'm gonna be in so much trouble..."

Elle Iverson

(*Sniff. Wipe away a tear. Sniff again.*)

"This was sup'sed to be just a quick pit stop before we toured the campus-". This time I let a sob catch in my throat, obviously unable to go on.

"Hey, hey, hey, it's ok." He pats my arm gently. He has kind eyes. "Can you call someone on the bus so they'll turn around?" He looks genuinely concerned.

I shake my head, "My teacher will be so ticked. I can't believe I was so stupid!" I stomp my foot and put my palm-to-forehead for effect. "I just need to get to the campus, or just close enough so I can walk there. I hate to bother you, but you look so much like my uncle, I felt like you might be able to help me…"

I can see his wheels spinning. Maybe he's figuring out if he has enough time. Maybe he's thinking about the risk of taking a girl alone in his truck. Maybe he's just trying to decide if he wants one piece of pizza or two… whatever question it was, he must've answered it because he replies, "Alright Darlin', let me pay for this here breakfast and I can run ya down there…. Name's Ray, by the way." He extends his hand, I shake it with both of mine.

"I'm Christina." I sniff and let out an exaggerated sigh to emphasize my relief. I hang back and let him select two pieces of pizza and I politely shake my head when he offers one to me. I'm starving but I can't risk the grease-soaked pizza upsetting my stomach. Not today.

He pays for his food and we head out the front door, which he holds for me. As I walk by him, I pull my phone from my back pocket, hit the blank screen twice and put it to my ear.

"Hey Landra, It's me." I say to no one. "I found a ride. It's a really nice guy named Ray. He looks exactly like my Uncle Chuck, even has the same beard…" I shoot Ray a smile. "He said he'll drop me off. Wait for me outside. We'll be in a semi with a red cab, there's a cross on the side and it says 'Heavenly Haulin'' above it. We should be there in about fifteen minutes… K. Bye." I said the spiel to myself but I did it loud enough so Ray doesn't get any ideas. Now he thinks someone is waiting for me who has

Avenged Innocence

a description of him and his truck. If he did have ulterior motives for helping me, the fake phone call should dissuade him from trying anything. He looks like a nice enough guy... but looks can be deceiving.

I should know.

I crawl into the passenger-side bucket seat, secure Pac between my legs, and leave my phone on my lap. I've been in a fair share of semis and Ray's is pretty run of the mill. A few coke bottles on the floorboard, a few wrappers in the windshield, and the faint smell of an old air freshener that is masked by the overriding 'lived-in' odor.

But what I pay attention to are the personal trinkets. You can tell a lot about a trucker by the cab of his rig.

Some guys have a gyrating Hawaiian dancer, some have fuzzy dice or a cross hanging from the rearview mirror, some have a poster of a pin-up girl from the 90s riding shotgun.

But most cabs I've been in are similar to Ray's. Photos and knickknacks to remind him of his family. Ray has pictures of the same five faces splayed on every bare surface of the dash. A homely-looking, middle-aged woman and four boys. There are a couple medals hanging from the rearview mirror and a beanie baby stuffed into the cup-holder closest to me. It's an owl that's positioned so it appears to be gazing up at Ray. It's cute.

Ray turns the key in the ignition and I'm not surprised to hear 'Ring of Fire' playing on the radio. That fits. I woulda pegged Ray as a Johnny Cash fan.

He puts the rig in gear and starts with the same question most of my conversations in trucks have started with, "So, where ya from?"

For all my faults, I try not to lie. Partly for moral reasons. My daddy always told us, 'You're only as good as your word.' And 'Liars never prosper.' And other such clichés. But I also try to be honest because half-truths are less risky than blatant lies; so that's the route I usually take.

"Minnesota. A little town south of The Cities. Where are you from?"

Another trick I learned early on is that people love to talk about themselves.

Remaining anonymous 101: Ask questions.

If people are talking about themselves then they're not asking about you.

The fewer questions I'm asked, the fewer chances I have to slip up.

Minimalizing risk, it's what I do.

"Oh, I'm from a little map dot just down the road. I only do short runs nowadays. I used to haul all over but my wife, Betty…" He motions toward the picture of the homely brunette. "She got tired of raisin' our boys on her own. That there's Owen, Andrew, Benny, and the youngest is Oliver; Ollie for short. Ollie was born when Benny was two years old. He thought we was callin' the baby Owly 'steada Ollie. Well now Ollie is purt near ten years old and I'll be a monkey's uncle if we don't still call him Owly. He gave me this here stuffed owl a couple years ago. Said he wanted me to always have Owly ridin' next to me when I was truckin'. Well, that along with my beautiful Betty's gentle naggin, is what spurred me to look for a route that would keep me close to home." He continues to ramble about his family and the change in his lifestyle now that he isn't driving 'all over tarnation'. I nod and interject 'uh-huh' and 'oh' where appropriate but I let my mind wander to my meeting. My obsession. My addiction. My purpose.

It's what I think about 24/7, at least now. It was harder at first. Harder not to think about my family and what they must have gone through. The first year on my own I cried. A lot. I felt bad for my mom and my brothers and I missed them. I still do… And I miss my daddy. I miss him so much there is a physical ache in my chest. He was my hero. Taken entirely too soon. The ache morphs to anger when I think about what happened. That single event that changed the course of my entire life. The ripple effects

Avenged Innocence

will be immeasurable. Not just my daddy, not just the core of my very being, but Mama and the boys.... What they have had to endure.

And now all the other families who will deal with loss.

Necessary or not, they still mourn. Their lives will never be the same. When the man of the house is removed, the whole family changes.

The first year after daddy died, we went to the cemetery every day. William was eleven. I was eight. Riker was only five years old and didn't understand why everyone was always crying.

I can see Mama splayed out as she wept on my daddy's grave. My brothers and I huddled under a tree, crying and holding each other.

I shake my head to clear the image.

Tears brim in my eyes. I wonder how Mama and the boys are doing now... No. Focus, Christina. Focus. The meeting. I need to concentrate on the task at hand. That's how I function.

That's how I survive.

Strict mental discipline.

I begin visualizing the next steps in my mind. Running through the checklist. Mentally scrolling through red flags to watch for. Rescripting plans for different scenarios. Playing them all out in my head.

As much as I'm blocking, as laser focused as I try to be, and even with Ray still going on about Owly being a prodigy eight-second rodeo star, I can't get the nagging question out of the back of my mind. It is the main reason why I don't let myself think about my family.

It always circles back to this.

The same question will drift to the forefront of my mind and overshadow my best efforts to block it out...

Does Mama splay herself on my grave too?

CHAPTER 5

Suddenly I can't wait to get out of the truck and into the fresh air. "Right here is good."

"You sure?" Ray, who had been mid-sentence when we pulled up to the red light, is puzzled.

"Yep. This is perfect. The gas station is only a couple blocks away." I open the door and sling Pac over my shoulder as I hop down and slip my phone securely in my back pocket.

"Thanks a lot. I really appreciate the lift." I smile and close the door just as the light turns green.

I hurry off the busy road and up the street to the gas station. Once again, I walk straight to the bathroom. I'm relieved it's completely vacant. I'm dizzy and a little nauseous. Not unusual for meeting day. It doesn't matter how many times I do this, I still get anxious. My heart beats faster. My palms get sweaty. My stomach feels like it's been tied in knots by a child who doesn't know how to tie their shoes yet, so they just wrap the laces round and round until enough slack is gone, resulting in an exaggerated obnoxious concoction of twists and loops.

I brace myself over the sink and stare into the mirror.

This is a pretty classic scene from the movies when the actor is trying to clear their head. I don't get it.

Looking intently at my reflection, especially when I'm high-school Christina, only conflicts my thoughts further.

Avenged Innocence

I segue to another classic movie-move; splashing water on my face. This is more effective. I repeat it a couple times. Letting the coldness of the water distract from the nervousness the rest of my body is exhibiting.

I take a couple deep breaths. In through the nose, out through the mouth, just like daddy taught me.

It's fine. I'm fine. Everything will be fine.

I have reason to be doubly paranoid.

I can't get caught.

And, just as importantly, I can't be recognized.

I reach to the bottom of Pac (in the compartment where my phone is usually stashed) and pull out a small metal Altoids container. I have a wallet in the front zipper pocket where I keep about twenty dollars and change, but this mint tin is my savings. I take out the bills and quickly thumb through them. I'm down to three hundred dollars. I peel off two ten dollar bills and shove them in my front pocket. I place the rest of the money back in the tin on top of the ATM card that's safely tucked into the bottom. I'm the only homeless person I know with a debit card…but, to be fair, I set it up in preparation for living on the street. I don't use it much. Actually only for the phone bill that is auto drafted each month.

Three hundred dollars is getting low and, if I remember correctly, my bank account only has enough for three more months of phone payments. I need this meeting to work out.

But that means I need to be extra diligent. Extra careful. I can't let my need for cash influence my decision.

I tuck everything back in its place, zip up Pac, and check my phone. Still plenty of time.

I use the ten dollar bill to buy two granola bars, a pack of bubble gum, and large Coke. I hate to spend the money but it's necessary to complete my look. The gas station clerks nods at me and smiles in recognition.

Darn it.

I smile back and grab my items. This'll be the last time I stop here. The campus is an ideal meeting spot but I can't run the risk of becoming memorable.

I make my way to the playground that is situated on the edge of the college campus. The area is beautiful, especially this time of year. Lots of tall trees and lush green grass. I pop a piece of bubble gum in my mouth and take a drink of the ice cold pop. Just another college kid out for a stroll.

An emergency vehicle siren sounds a little ways off and my heart stops. For such a common occurrence, the shrill sound still stops me in my tracks every time. Literally. I stop walking and stand frozen in the middle of the sidewalk while my mind flashes back to my father pulling up in his rig on my 8th birthday. The sirens were blaring. He was smiling from ear to ear, holding Jewely behind his back. (Pronounced Julie but spelled differently since the pink teddy bear had emerald colored stones for eyes and ruby chips lining her ears. I thought I was quite clever with Jewely. I was eight, give me a break.) Daddy had told me that he wouldn't be able to come to my party because he had to work. I had been disappointed but tried not to show it because Daddy was a hero. When he was at work he was saving lives. Plus, he always came home and told me about his adventures.

Until the one time he didn't.

I feel a hot tear slide down my cheek.

Not again.

Focus, Christina. Dang it. Why had I let myself reminisce this morning? Why had I let my mind wander? Today of all days.
When I let thoughts of my previous life creep in, even if it's just for a little bit, it's so much harder to block them out afterwards.

I concentrate on putting one foot in front of the other and walking at a normal pace. I welcome the butterflies that are starting to flutter. The closer I get to the playground, the more my anxiety builds. It's much more enjoyable than sadness.

Four years. I don't know how many first meetings. Maybe a hundred? But only six transactions.

Avenged Innocence

Transactions. That's what I call them.

And this could lead to number seven.

Everything seems to add up so far, but I have to be careful not to let my low funds skew my judgement. I still need to be thorough. Dot all the i's and cross all the t's. There is probably a few weeks' worth of work to do to make sure my newest possibility is legit... but so far he meets all the criteria.

#1. He reached out to me.

#2. He mentioned Pez (street name for Oxy).

#3. He suggested the meeting.

Only one more box to check.

I can see the park clearly now. This location is perfect for meetings because it's usually bustling with activity.

We're supposed to meet at the monkey bars. I find a spot in the grass, near a couple blonde girls who look to be about my age. Both of them are on their phones. Both have drinks. Both are wearing sunglasses.

Both are chewing gum.

I drop Pac next to them.

"Emily?" I ask the girl closest to me.

She turns her head up from her phone. "Ummm. No."

"Ohmigosh, I'm so sorry. You look just like my old roommate." I crouch down next to Pac, assumedly get a better look at her face. She lifts her glasses, revealing that she is not my fictitious previous roommate.

I offer her an embarrassed smile.

"I'm sorry. I didn't mean to bother you. I guess I was just excited there was someone here I could crash next to."

"Oh, no worries."

Now it's her turn to smile. She is pretty. "Feel free." She extends her hand to the patch of grass in front of Pac.

"Oh, thank you so much!"

"I'm Marissa," she offers, "and this is Kathy."

"Christina." I smile, whip my phone out of my pocket and plop down in front of Pac. I fish my earbuds out of the side zipper. I lean back, prop one foot on my knee, plug the earbuds into my phone and stick one in my ear and let the other hang down. I take a drink of Coke and open a granola bar. I pretend to turn my full attention to my phone and I become invisible. Another college girl, zoning out, soaking up some sun.

I look around, from behind the shield of my sunglasses, and study the other occupants of the playground. There are quite a few college kids, a few young mothers pushing children on the swings, and a group of teenagers a little ways out playing football. My eyes drift over a young couple, they've got to be in their mid-teens. Maybe fifteen? Sixteen? They're laying on a blanket under a tree, giggling. They're both a little awkward.

The boy, a wanna-be type with shaggy brown hair, moves to brush a strand of hair from the girl's face. Her hair, the same shade as his and barely a few inches longer, is loosely tied up in a messy bun on top of her head. She's self-consciously using one arm to cover her stomach, which is visible thanks to the crop top she's wearing. She's dressing to impress but lacking confidence.

From their body language, they haven't *been together* yet.

He is fidgety. Playing with the extra fabric from his goliath-sized belt cinching his baggy pants around his tiny waist. Constantly flipping his hair and obnoxiously popping his knuckles.

She's laughing too much and chewing on her fingernails.

Yeah. They haven't slept together yet. But soon.

They say you always remember your first time.

I suppose that's true for everyone. But my first time, while etched in my memory, is not just memorable. It changed me. Fundamentally. Forever.

Occasionally I'll wonder if things had been different, if I had not gone to the park that day, would I be normal now? Or was this outcome inevitable?

But it's foolish to suppose. The fact is that I did go to the park that day. I did, at only twelve-years-old, follow the fifteen-year-old boy into the woods. He had enticed me with a story about

Avenged Innocence

kittens hiding under a bush. I had believed him. He was cute. At twelve, I was just starting to have crushes and pay attention to boys.

I knew about sex… functionally. What went where and how babies were made.

But my visions about love involved feather kisses and handholding.

I was naïve walking into the woods.

I was a completely different person walking out.

CHAPTER 6

I still have thirty minutes before meeting time so I scan the park looking for anything suspicious and for anyone who may be looking for 'me'. Or the nine-year-old version of me they think will be showing up.

'Lilly' is who I am meeting. She said she'd be here with her dad. She'll be wearing shorts and a t-shirt. Her dad always wears a red ball cap and usually some sort of Mavericks basketball shirt.

I met 'Lilly' online.

'Lilly' is clever.

'Lilly' is a pedophile.

This is what I do.

I catch perverts.

My routine is far from flawless but it has served me well and I continue to tweak it when necessary.

I like to keep it simple.

I have profiles on multiple social media accounts, all different names, and all pretty generic. I'm usually nine years old but can go up or down a couple years.

My favorite app (the one where I met 'Lilly') is PlayRound.

The initial concept itself is fine. The premise is to give kids a positive and safe social media experience.

You create an avatar. (Mine is a unicorn named Darcy who has a rainbow striped horn and wears a tiara.) When someone

Avenged Innocence

approaches you in the app, then a little blurb pops up above the avatar's head. It lists your hobbies, favorite movies, and things you're good at... so you'll be able to see what you have in common with each other. You can provide your city and state but anything more specific than that is banned, for safety reasons.

You walk your avatar around an elaborate playground where you can play different games on the equipment, join games that are going on, and compliment the other avatars.

Absolutely no bullying allowed.

And, every time you log on, there is a stop sign reminder that warns users not to reveal any personal information and never, ever meet in person. Ever.

Because kids always listen to warnings.

But what does ring true is that very few kids will reach out to someone they don't know. Internet safety is a huge trigger nowadays. Parents and teachers are diligent about warning kids (to the point of scaring them) about the dangers online.

The ones who usually reach out to a nine-year-old girl who logs online at 3:00, right after school, are perverts like 'Lilly'.

Well, 'Lilly' is Paul.

I don't know his real name yet. Paul is an acronym I came up with for Perverted And Undeserving Loser. I use acronyms for all my targets. (Jewely, Pac, Paul; I'm pretty clever with word play.)

It's almost shocking how smooth these guys are.

Paul, for example, chatted with me a couple times a week (under the guise of Lilly, a ten-year-old girl) for almost a month before telling me that 'she' met a new friend at school named Darcy. That's when 'Lilly' asked for my picture. 'She' wanted to see if I was the same girl. Unfortunately, my parents had disabled the camera on my iPad.

The conversations continued. Getting more and more familiar until Lilly suggested meeting. This is where I slow play. My mommy and daddy don't allow me to meet up with anyone from online. But through the course of the conversations we've already had, the creeper on the other side of the screen knows that my

Elle Iverson

mommy and daddy are getting divorced and I'm mad at them. He will use that. His parents will be divorced too... or at least fighting a lot. After all, I just need a friend to relate with. It'd be totally neat to meet face to face and just talk.

I wait a little longer before finally agreeing to meet.

Once the meeting happens, and I know that the person on the other end will result in a transaction, then I won't use that avatar anymore. I'll keep it to communicate with him but I won't use it to meet with anyone else. Safety first.

So far, no one hanging out at the playground looks out of place. The young couple has gathered their blanket and moved on; their spot is now occupied by the sweaty football players taking a break.

There is a guy standing against a tree who seems to be watching them. But then I see his gaze shift towards us and it slows down when he gets to my pretty new friends. He seems to study the girls for a second before he realizes he is staring. Then he turns and begins walking toward the slides. Another run of the mill middle-aged dude looking to score a college chick.

A red ball cap catches my eye. I see a tall man wearing the signature hat and a Mavericks t-shirt walking toward the playground. He is clean cut and average build. He is nondescript.

He looks...nice.

He is not with a child.

He walks over to a slide and leans against it as he eyes the monkey bars.

Why hello Paul.

I watch him from behind my sunglasses without moving my head.

He got here early too. He walks the perimeter of the playground, smiling and waving to the parents pushing their kids on swings. I can tell he's also scanning. Looking for out-of-place work trucks that could be a command center for a sting operation. Glancing at ears for microphones and looking at anyone sitting alone. I watch his gaze drift over Non-Fictitious-

<u>Avenged Innocence</u>

Emily's friend, Non-Fictitious-Emily, and me but he doesn't even pause. Why would he? Three blonde co-eds enjoying a break from classes is one of the reasons this park exists.

I watch him continue to circle the area. Appearing nonchalant.

My nervousness is slowly being replaced with excitement.

I'm waiting, willing him to do it. Check off the next box for me.

Thirty minutes pass quickly and he lingers next to the monkey bars, looking around, watching for someone who's not coming.

He jams his hand in his pockets.

C'mon. C'mon.

Do it.

His hand comes out of his pocket and I hold my breath.

Nope, just his phone.

He fiddles with it for a minute before sliding it back into his pocket. His other hand emerges from the other pocket, holding a pill bottle.

He pops the lid off and tosses a small white tablet in his mouth.

Bingo.

He just checked off box #4. He's a user. Which probably means he's an addict.

I wait a few minutes and enjoy watching him sweat.

He's a nice-looking guy, clean shaven, short hair.

This will be fun.

I wish I could call it vigilante justice (and I guess part of it could be) but the truth is that it's an outlet for my own addiction.

I think of it as a healthy release.

Like if a glutton only ate vegetables.

Or if a sex addict only carried out fantasies with their spouse.

It's not a great compulsion to have, and like most addictions eventually do, it has cost me everything.

CHAPTER 7

Ok, I've waited long enough. I open the Uber app and request a ride. For destination location I put in one of the malls that is about twenty minutes away, even though I don't really know where I'm going.

Now the timing gets tricky. When Paul starts to pace away, looking like he's ready to leave, I open up the PlayRound app. I click the messaging icon and type, 'Sry my mom came home'.

I hit send and sit back to watch. I see him pull out his phone. A look that is mixture of relief and disappointment crosses his face. I see him tapping on his screen. He's still oblivious to me. I pretend to be doing something else on my phone while I wait for his reply. I glance up and see him staring at the phone in his hand. Trying to figure out what to say?

He begins typing again and a message flashes across my screen. 'Ok. Tmrw?'

'Can't. Going to my dads.'

'Next week?'

'Sure. Same place?'

'Y'

'K'

I see him scan across the playground one more time.
Probably out of habit more than precaution.

Avenged Innocence

I stand up and say a cheerful goodbye to the girls who had served as my camouflage. They dismiss me quickly but I loiter, fiddling with my phone, waiting for Paul to leave.

I breathe a sigh of relief when he slips his phone in his pocket and walks away from the campus. I slowly head that way as well.

I had hoped (and planned) that he would park over here. It's where my Uber is being sent.

There are tall bushes that line the street and separate the park from the road. Good cover and discreet. Not that he would have nabbed the little girl unsuspectingly from the monkey bars. No, he's too clever for that. He would have found his target, approached her warmly, and explained that his daughter was already at the house waiting, she had stayed home with her mom to make fresh baked cookies for their special afternoon.

Mentioning the mom and cookies adds warmth and security.

So the little girl would willingly walk with him. The bushes were appealing to him because they would hide his car on the off-chance someone recognized the little girl later on; when she winds up missing.

He is a nobody. He blends in. There is nothing remarkable about it.

At least not on the surface.

Underneath, he is evil. I can sense the darkness.

I have an ability to see past facades and into intentions.

I have a gift for identifying the dark desires in others.

I think that I'm uniquely suited for detecting violence since I was exposed to it at such a young age.

The evil my young soul saw, melded something inside me.

But the question I have wrestled with every day for the past seven years is: Was I born this way or did the instance in the clearing of those woods make me this way?

I want to know if this was who I was always supposed to be or if circumstances created the person I am now.

I've read studies about how children of alcoholics can be predisposition to addiction.

My parents were phenomenal. Neither one drank.

But maybe there was a gene deep down that was passed on.

Or maybe it was a combination of timing and age that resulted in the perfect storm to create this desire in me.

Either way, it is what got me here.

This addiction.

I check my phone and my Uber is still in route.

Dang it.

I fall a little further behind Paul and cut across the open green space. According to my phone, I'm looking for a silver minivan being driven by a guy named Pendar. That's good. In this part of town there's a huge chance of getting college kids as a driver. If it's a girl, they like to talk. If it's a guy, they like to flirt. I'm not in the mood for either.

Pendar looks like he's in his forties.

Paul slips into a black Nissan Maxima.

My heart starts to beat faster. No sign of Pendar. Then I see his van round the corner. I turn my back to Paul and pray that he stalls long enough for me to get situated and follow him. I walk briskly towards Pendar. I don't even wait for the van to come to a complete stop before I pull on the sliding door. It's locked, obviously, since the car is still in gear.

Cool your jets, Christina.

Pendar unlocks the door and I can tell he is already annoyed.

Awesome.

He looks older in person. He's probably fifty. He has graying hair and his car smells of body odor.

I shift into character right away.

"I'm sorry. I know I said I'm going to the mall but the truth is I don't know where I'm going. I'm following my boyfriend because my friend told me he's married. He's in that black Maxima."

Again, half-truths... Well, this is more like quarter-truth but still not an outright lie. I am following the guy.

Avenged Innocence

I throw Pac on the floorboard and assume the role of distraught girlfriend. I watch Pendar's expression melt from annoyance, to consideration, to determination.

"Where does he live?" He's putting the car in gear. The black car turns right onto a one-way. Pendar follows.

"I don't know. We never went to his house. Always my apartment… I can't believe I was this stupid… Thank you for your help." I slouch back into the seat, feigning defeat while actually calculating my next move.

The black Maxima is heading to the interstate. He probably lives in a nearby town. And now I'll know exactly where so it becomes easier to follow him. This is one of the hardest parts, trailing him after the meeting.

Pendar asks a question. I don't hear what he says but instead of asking him to repeat it, I fake a sob. This was a fairly easy manipulation to master.

Over the years, even before I became Christina, I had to learn to emulate emotions I wasn't actually feeling.

We're in the car for a while; it seems even longer because Pendar doesn't have the radio on. Finally, we follow Paul into a small gated community. According to the giant stone displayed at the entrance, it's called Aspen Views.

In the middle of Texas.

Okay.

Whatever.

I solidify my troubled mistress façade by adding a quiver to my voice as Paul pulls into a driveway about a block ahead of us. He parks next to a maroon minivan. It seems like there's always a minivan.

As we drive past the large blue house, I don't look at it. Instead, I study the neighborhood. There was a commercial area a couple miles back and if this suburb is like all the others, there will be a cluster of fast food places not far away.

Pendar pulls to a stop. This wasn't as far as I thought it might be but it's far enough that I will use all my cash.

"You can stop here. This is fine. I need to walk."

I can sense Pendar's hesitation. Crazy girlfriend confronts cheating married man… not a lot of good outcomes.

I look him in the eyes through the rearview mirror.

"I'm fine. I'm not mad, I'm just disappointed." A classic line used by parents, spouses, and homeless stalkers.

The digital wage thingamabob says I owe him $23. I've already run the risk of having a memorable story; I don't need to be remembered as being a lousy tipper too. I hand him the full $30.

"I can wait around. Give you a ride back to the city… free of charge."

"No, I'm ok. Really. But thank you."

I give him, what I hope is, a reassuring smile as I haul Pac out and fling it over my shoulder.

I slide the door shut and turn to survey the area.

The nervousness is gone. I made it undetected and unnoticed.

Now comes the fun part.

Casing the joint.

CHAPTER 8

For some reason 'Every Breath You Take' by The Police pops into my head and I mutter the lyrics as I walk towards Paul's house. Instead of turning to pass in front of his place, I look both ways and cross the street while making sure his car is still in the driveway.

I circle around the block in front of his house and look both ways again when crossing back. His car is still there. Now to scope out the block behind his house.

There are a few for-sale signs, and one of them is placed on an out-of-control lawn.

Nothing stands out. Nothing out of the ordinary. But that's usual.

There is a small play area a little further into the neighborhood that has a swing set and a slide but it's not busy enough for me to blend in.

Now that I've gotten the lay of the land, I'll risk walking by the front of Paul's house. Just once. It's a nice house with a two-car garage, big bushes in the front and a small window in the pointed easement of the attic.

Quaint.
Cute.
Normal.

Elle Iverson

I memorize the street and house number. These houses already look a lot alike. Factor in the car being gone and darkness setting in and it would be pretty easy to get them mixed up. As I walk by I also look at the license plate of the Maxima. The house number is 445. License plate number is 508.

445 House. 508 plate.

I continue to repeat them in a singsong voice while I make my way out of the subdivision.

Aspen Views. Pffft. Granted, I didn't walk the whole area but in the parts I did, I sure didn't see any views other than houses on one side and tumbleweeds on the other.

Now, how am I gonna play this?

Should I walk back towards the commercial area and try to find a place to set up a temporary camp? Or should I venture the other direction and hope there's something there? Some place for cover.

Better play it safe. It's getting late. I think it was only a few miles to the business area but I could be wrong. I need to try to get back before dark to scope it out. I should have been paying closer attention when Pendar was driving.

Oh well, I'll hightail it there and keep my fingers crossed that I can find some place to bed down for the night.

I can use the walk to think.

I'm not sure how long I'll have to follow Paul. It all depends on him. I'm about ninety percent sure he's gonna be a go.

He showed up at a playground (that was way out of his neighborhood) expecting to meet a nine-year-old and he popped a pill when he was nervous.

Now I need to figure out where he works, where he gets his drugs, and where I can catch him off-guard.

The movies and TV crime shows make stakeouts look easy. My mom used to watch Law and Order (like, all of them) and whenever they needed to keep tabs on someone they would park a work van on the street or send an undercover cop (dressed in overalls) up a telephone pole. I don't have a work van, or any car

Avenged Innocence

for that matter, and these newer developments don't even have telephone poles. My point is: This isn't easy. I don't have high-tech listening devices. I don't have binoculars.

I can't even casually stroll by because I have enormous army luggage strapped to my back.

The advantage I do have is that I grew up in a neighborhood like this. My methods are less high-tech, more risky, and more time-consuming.

As much as I love to plan, it's almost impossible to do any prep work for what will happen after the meeting until after the actual meeting. Then I have to act quickly.

At least there's a busy business area close by. I've had a couple meetings that didn't pan out because the potential transaction lived in the middle of nowhere. Not that it would've been impossible to watch... but because it isn't safe for me.

Ok, maybe not unsafe, but creepy.

There's something about hunkering down in the woods, surrounded by snakes and spiders that creeps me out. For starters; I watched 'Arachnophobia' with my older cousins when I was far too young. They were babysitting and it came on TV. My parents were out of town and my brothers and I were staying with our Aunt and Uncle who were also out for the evening. They had left my teenage cousins to babysit. To their credit, they tried to send me to bed. But I whined and complained until they finally agreed to let me stay up and watch the movie with them. I was terrified but didn't want to look like a baby so I sat through the whole thing. I blame my fear of spiders on that.

As for snakes; there was that time we were camping at a small lake. We usually headed home before it got dark but the fish were biting and mom and dad were distracted by telling us stories of their dating adventures (my dad worked really hard to impress my mom, sometimes it had hilarious outcomes) and before we knew it, it was dusk. I vividly remember my dad's eyes getting wide and him telling us to hurry and reel in our lines. As I peered across the lake, it looked like oil fingers covering the dark blue water.

Snakes were coming out of every corner and from under every tree. As we gathered our supplies, I remember thinking how snakes had been surrounding us that whole time and I never knew it.

Ironic, knowing what I know now.

As anxious as I am for planning the next steps with Paul, I need to shift gears and figure out my living situation. The area I'm heading to has a few warehouses and a factory of some sort along with eating establishments. I'll try to find a quiet ally to rest. Preferably one with three of the sides closed in so no one can sneak up on me.

I'm wishing upon wish that I'll luck out and Paul works in one of these buildings. That will make my life so much easier.

As I approach the commercial area, I shimmy up an underpass for a wardrobe change. Time for college-Christina to switch back to homeless-Christina.

When I get to the top, I hunch over and pull Pac next to me. It feels good to sit. Today has been busy.

I check my phone one last time; seven-thirty p.m. but no new messages. I hide it back in its spot in the bottom of Pac. My fingers brush against my savings account and I remember I used all my cash to pay Pendar. I take out two more ten dollar bills to replenish my wallet. I change my clothes one article at a time. A few cars speed past but I don't think I'm noticeable. Even if I am, no one bothers to stop.

My nose crinkles when I open the baggie that contains my clothes from this morning.

Ugh. I don't like this part. I'll be fine in a few minutes but it takes a little while to adjust back to my smell. In addition to my baggy jeans and t-shirt, the wardrobe also features a pink bandana and (what were probably white but are now grayish-brown) sneakers.

I take off my sunglasses and pull out my hair-tie. I toss those in before zipping up the 'college' baggie.

Avenged Innocence

I run my fingers through my hair to dishevel the braid. I tie the bandana on top of my head in an Aunt Jemima fashion to hide the fact that my hair is not gross and greasy…yet.

I glance around to double check everything is in the correct place, then I scurry down to the road and head towards the rows of street lights that are just coming on.

The transformation only took minutes and just like that; College Christina is gone.

But she was never really there.

I suppose there may have been a version of her in my younger self… This long in, it's hard for me to tell which one is the real me.

The last few years I spent with my family I was restless and discontent.

Now I'm at home being homeless. I have my routines (though the location changes) and I have my rules. There is a certain level of comfort that comes with living with no comforts.

I am able to fully concentrate on my life's purpose. I can safely feed my addiction without worrying about hurting those closest to me. I don't get distracted by material things like having a fancy car or a nice place to live. My days are intentional.

Not many nineteen-year-olds can say that.

Yes, I'm proud of myself. I am happy.

And as long I keep repeating that, I am ok.

CHAPTER 9

I hear children laughing.

I smell grass and flowers. I'm wearing a simple white dress. I feel the soft blanket underneath me.

I'm lying on my side with one arm draped over my stomach, the other propped under my head, facing a good-looking guy.

Derek.

He says something funny and I laugh. My hair falls in my face and he gently uses one finger to tuck it behind my ear, the other one trails along my cheek. His touch gives me goosebumps all over, it makes my breathing shallow, and sets a fire in my belly.

I gaze into his eyes. They are filled with humor and mischief.

The breeze tickles my legs and I slide one over the other. I see him look. I watch his eyes slowly glide back up to meet mine. The mischief is still there but the humor has been replaced with desire. He is staring at me intently. He brings his hand back to my face but this time he cups my cheek and pulls me into him.

His eyes close as he leans towards me. I close my eyes and inhale.

His scent is hypnotizing. It excites me.

Every one of my nerves is alert. My body feels so alive.

Just before his lips touch mine, the sky opens up and it begins to rain.

Avenged Innocence

Derek laughs. The humor is back in his eyes and is now etched all over his face. He rolls me off the blanket, flinging it over his shoulders, creating a tent for us.

I sit down next to him.

He wraps one arm around me; the other is holding our blanket structure in place.

Again I breathe in the smell of him. This time I lay my head on his shoulder, completely content. I close my eyes and let the smile of a teenager in love play on my lips.

But the rain is still pelting me in the face. I try to snuggle deeper into Derek's side but now his warm body is cold and hard as a rock. His clothes scratch against my cheek.

I open my eyes and the musky manly smell of Derek that had driven me crazy is replaced by the familiar stench of garbage. It drives me crazy too… but in a completely different way.

I had been using Pac as a pillow and the material scratches my cheek. I sit up, pulling my knees to my chest. The rain is coming down harder now. I scoot closer to the dumpster, trying to find shelter in the lid that's flipped open, which is creating a slight overhang.

I made it safely to the commercial area last night but it had taken longer than I anticipated so it was already dark when I arrived. There hadn't been much time to scout around. I had hoped to do that today but it looks like it'll have to wait. Along with the other unknowns when homeless, weather plays a huge part in determining plans and tasks for the day. I need to see if there's a community nearby. I need to figure out where I can get presentable and, more importantly, where I can get some food.

But all that will have to wait until the torrential downpour passes.

I grab the last gas station granola bar from Pac's side zipper and let my mind replay the dream.

Derek.

I don't believe in soulmates but I do believe in true love. Derek was my first and (to-date) my only love.

His family lived two houses down on our cul-de-sac. His mom and my mom were both social workers and were best friends. This meant that we spent a lot of time together. Derek was two years older than me, one year younger than my older brother, William. At first, he was only William's friend. But they would let me play with them if I fussed enough.

When my daddy died, I was eight and Derek was ten. He proved to be a great friend. Most people don't know how to act or what to say when you're going through the worst tragedy one can imagine. I heard a lot about how much daddy loved me, though I already knew that. I heard a lot of "I'm so sorry" which annoyed me. If you didn't kill him why are you apologizing? It's not your fault he's gone.

The one response I could hardly stand was 'He's in a better place'. Whether or not that was true, at eight years old, I wanted my daddy with me. Happily holding me while kissing my mama and high-fiving my brothers. I wanted him here.

Derek didn't offer any platitudes. He also didn't pretend like my daddy never existed, which a lot of people started to do, especially after a few months passed. No one wanted to mention his name or refer to him at all. As if talking about him would remind me that he was dead. I knew that. I thought about it almost every minute of every day. Avoiding talking about him, or purposefully not saying his name, didn't help. It made me think they were trying to make me forget about him.

But Derek would talk about my daddy. And he would let me talk about my daddy. And he would let me cry.

Eventually we also talked about other things. We found out that we had a lot in common. We continued to hang out until I was eleven and he was thirteen. Then we 'dated' for nine months... until his parents divorced and his mom moved back to her hometown in rural Minnesota. His dad sold the house and moved to an apartment in the cities.

Avenged Innocence

I will never forget standing in our backyard, holding hands, saying goodbye. I could tell he wanted to kiss me... but we had never done that; and we never would.

His mom hollered that they were loading up. He looked at me with those crystal clear eyes, squeezed my hand, and pecked me on the cheek.

"Goodbye Aurora." He whispered and then he left.

That was the second worst day of my life.

At least it was at the time.

Six months later it would drop to third.

The rain shows no signs of letting up. The heavy droplets cascade around me and blow onto Pac. There is a Burger King a couple blocks away. I need a hot meal and it will be nice to get out of the rain. I wait for a break from the downpour and race back the direction I came in last night. I wasn't able to see much then but today I'll be able to root around some more.

I make it to BK just as the sky opens up and a sheet of water drenches me.

I scurry to the bathroom. I walk in and stand in front of the mirror. Not College Christina and not Homeless Christina but something more reminiscent of a drowned rat.

I'm torn. On one hand, I really need to use my phone (and thanks to Mother Nature's shower I could put myself together pretty easily and pull off the college look) but on the other hand, I'll probably be camping out here for a while. I can't risk being seen 'done-up' and with a phone...

I compromise. I check all the stalls to make sure I'm alone and then I take a couple minutes to freshen up. I brush my teeth, comb my hair, and fix the bandana. Then I head to the handicap stall, set Pac on the built-in changing table, and take out my phone.

I hold down the power button to turn it on.

I let my pants fall to my ankles and I perch on the side of the toilet. If anyone comes in, it'll just look like I'm having some 'issues'.

The screen comes to life and the first thing I check is the perv-finding app.

I click through the red warning that pops up saying that I agree to the rules and will heed the caution.

My unicorn, Darcy, is holding three envelopes.

I've got mail.

The envelopes each have a picture of the senders' avatars on the front.

As I suspected, the first one is a yellow teddy bear with a pink bow…That's Paul.

The next one is a chicken with a red bowtie, that's Gus. (Gross Unsuspecting Scumbag)

I've been chatting with him a few weeks too. He's suggested meeting twice now. If Paul falls through I just may take him up on it.

I can only handle one transaction at a time.

So many pedophiles. So little time.

The third envelope has a picture of a blue bunny wearing sunglasses and over-the-ear headphones. I haven't seen him before.

Hmmmm.

I'm curious but I force myself to close the app without reading any of the messages. It's eight-thirty in the morning. I should be in school right now. The app shows the sender when their mail was read. I'm diligent about only being active from three to five o'clock in the evening when I'm home from school. Alone.

The door to the bathroom opens. I hear someone enter the stall next to mine and I see black pants drop down over black sneakers. An employee. I need to hurry.

But one more thing…

I google the closest library.

Avenged Innocence

It's three miles away and a pretty straight shot.
Perfect.
I can walk that in an hour.
Then I remember the rain. I can't afford to Uber again. I also can't afford to risk coming up with a hitchhiking story if this is where I'm going to be living.
I decide to pull an audible. I grab the bag holding my 'extra outfit' and take out the shirt. It's a form-fitting plain white tee. I hear the water turn on and I say a silent 'thank you' that the employee is washing her hands. I switch out my oversized homeless shirt for the white one. I turn off my phone and flush the toilet. I secure my phone in its hiding place and step out of my stall as the bathroom door closes behind the employee.
I use the hand dryer to dry my large gray shirt that is still a little wet from the rain and shove it in the correct bag. I also lose the bandana and whip my hair into two Pippi Longstocking type braids. Only instead of sticking straight out to the sides, they lay on my shoulders, resting right above the black outline of my bra.
I swing Pac on my shoulders and hurry out of the bathroom and to the counter.
A sausage, egg, and cheese biscuit is calling my name.

CHAPTER 10

I get my breakfast order and sit at a table by a window. The rain is still coming down and the whole sky is gray. The air looks thick. As much as this weather messes up my agenda, I still love it. Something about the dreariness is comforting.

On bright sunshiny days when the rest of the world is happy, when I see the smiles, when I feel the sun, when I can hear laughter, it makes me think of my family. That's when I miss my old life.

But in the rain, the drear, the mundane, my current life fits better. It's easier for me to focus on my job. My purpose. Easier for me to plan for my transactions.

Like today.

First: I need to get to the library. I actually spend quite a bit of time in libraries. They are dry. They are temperature-controlled. Conversations (aka questions) are discouraged and there's free Wi-Fi. Ideally I would use the library computers but since you need a library card to log on (and you need an address to get a library card) I'll settle for using my phone. Plus, library computers would pinpoint location and browsing history when I check PlayRound. No, my phone is safer.

My cell phone plan is the cheapest I could find so it only has a small data package. (Another reason the campus playgrounds are good meeting spots; the college broadband usually reaches.)

Avenged Innocence

Second: At the library I have a laundry list of things I need to research; starting with Paul's real name. That should be pretty simple now that I know his address and license plate number. Once I know his identity I might be able to find out where he works and figure out the best way to follow him.

Third: I need a home base. The dumpster corner I slept in last night won't do. It was unprotected and exposed. I need to find a new group to huddle up with. If I get to the library soon, that'll give me a couple hours to snoop around. Then at three o'clock, I can catch up on my creeper correspondence and be back to this area before dark to find a place to crash.

And now I have the plan.

Thanks to my hippy grudge look (baggy jeans and tight white shirt) hopefully I'll get a ride seamlessly and I won't stand out once I get there.

I finish off my sandwich and crumple the wrapper. I swallow the last bit of water and toss the cup and wrapper into the garbage can on my way out the door.

I'm surprised (and relieved) to see the rain has slowed to a drizzle. It's still wet but more manageable.

According to google maps the library is straight down this road and one block over.

Unfortunately it's the opposite direction from Paul's house.

I'm currently in the middle of a busy area. In addition to the BK, there's a 7-Eleven, a Taco Bell, a Tire and Lube Express, a car wash, and a grocery store. A centralized cell for the surrounding communities so they don't have to venture all the way to the suburbs.

A suburb of the suburbs, if you will.

A red four-door Camry stops on the way out of the 7-Eleven and when the window rolls down I see an attractive man in his early thirties.

"Need a lift?" This was the response I had been banking on when I switched out my shirt.

"Oh… thanks." I act surprised by the offer and reply, "It's okay, I'm actually just heading to the library." I roll my eyes back to Pac and shrug my shoulders. "Homework." I say the word with the resigned-ness of a frustrated (but polite) teenager.

Oh the stresses of geography and social studies.

"It's on my way." He smiles and nods, motioning for me to get in.

I hear the doors unlock and I walk around the car and open the door to the backseat of the passenger side. I throw Pac in first. It makes sense for me to ride back here because Pac is so big (all those school books, ya'know) but it's also a safety precaution. If the driver has a gun or knife, it's easier for him to use it on someone riding in the passenger seat.

You probably think I'm paranoid.

I probably am.

But I can't be too careful. I can't help but think of the worst case scenario in every situation. That's the way my brain works. I see the potential for danger. I see the easiest targets. I assume the worst in people. It makes for a somewhat lonely life but it's one of the reasons I can do what I do.

Patience, perspective, and the mentality that I'm living in an episode of Criminal Minds.

My handsome chauffer doesn't seem too interested in small talk. He's focused on navigating through the busy streets. The rain seems to slow things down. I glance at his hands resting on the steering wheel. No wedding ring. No car seats or sippy cups on the floorboard. No kids.

The car has a faint peppermint smell and he has the air-conditioning going so it feels breezy. A nice contrast to the heaviness of outside. Dave Matthew's Band is drifting from the speakers but is barely audible. The song fades out and the recognizable opening notes of 'Beat It' come on.
My driver turns the volume up for the King of Pop.

He seems normal.

Avenged Innocence

But after about ten minutes of silence I start to get nervous. Most people need to chatter. They need to fill the air with noise. This guy hasn't said a word since the initial greeting. I'm not the type to get uncomfortable in silence but I do get apprehensive when I'm around someone else who also isn't uncomfortable in silence.

"I really appreciate the lift."

"No problem." He shoots me a smile over his shoulder.

It looks genuine. That's unsettling.

I check my door and the child-lock is engaged.

My heart starts to beat faster and my mind races.

Stay calm.

The same anxiety that filled me in Ray's truck yesterday is back in full force and intensified.

I envision my thirty-something chauffer driving me to a deserted road. Pulling a gun on me, forcing himself on top of me… the panic explodes in my belly.

No.

I will not be a victim.

Not again.

I casually slip my bandana from the side of Pac and lay it length ways on my lap. I roll it up tightly so it forms a long rope.

I'll give him five more minutes or until we pass the library, then I'll slide behind him, wrap my bandana around his throat and twist it until I crush his windpipe. I'll brace myself into the seat and run as soon as the car stops.

I take a couple deep breaths.

Ok, that's the plan. I turn my head to look out the window but I cut my eyes to see him.

He's looking at me in the rearview mirror.

My heart stops.

My body tenses and I turn to pounce.

"Here we are." The smile is back and his eyes seem bright, almost dancing. "Opps, sorry about that, I always forget about those locks." He pushes a button and the door unlocks. I throw it open and put one leg out safely on the asphalt. I have my bandana in one hand, I grab Pac with the other, and mumble a 'thank you' as I shut the door behind me.

My heartbeat and blood pressure both return to normal pretty quickly.

This is my life.

Living out the worst case scenario at all times.

It gets exhausting.

I push that out of my mind as I head up the elegant path to the library.

I have more important things to work on now.

CHAPTER 11

I slide back in my chair and roll my neck.

Hours of Internet scrounging have paid off.

Paul's name is actually Richard Edmonson, but according to his Facebook profile, he goes by Richie.

A grown man... Richie.

He is from Dallas. He and his wife, Gretchen, have two daughters; Haylee is three and Katee just turned one. The happy couple has been married for five years.

He works at an accounting firm, Anderson Accounting Co, and she stays home with the kids.

The Internet really does offer up so much information.

It's not an in-depth search; no pulling credit card receipts or phone records. I'm a nineteen-year-old junior high drop out. It's simple social media stalking.

A backwards search of the address had given me his name. I quickly set up a phony profile as a mom in my thirties. I threw on a couple images of smiling kids as my profile pictures and then friend requested a bunch of Richie and Gretchen's mutual friends from the area. Once four or five of them accepted me, I sent a request to the target couple. Seeing that we had mutual friends, both accepted within an hour. Then it was just a matter of scrolling through their timelines to piece together a typical week.

It looks like Gretchen is pretty active with the girls. Swim lessons on Tuesday and Thursday mornings. A 'Mommy and Me' group on Wednesdays and most Mondays they are at the library for story time.

Richie isn't as active online as his wife is but his other feeds elude that he eats lunch downtown almost every day.

He's never 'checked in' to a gym and he's not a member of any groups associated with one. No races, no Iron Man courses. It's a small reassurance that he's not bulking up.

He looked thin from a distance and that can work to my advantage.

Is there anything I'm missing?

I lean back, stretching my hands above my head and rolling my neck again.

I had picked a single table in the back corner, right by a window and next to an outlet so I could plug in my phone charger. The rain has stopped but it's still overcast and dark.

I shift my eyes away from the rolling gray clouds and glance over the other library occupants. I have been so engrossed in my research I haven't paid attention to anyone around me.

About ten feet away, beside another window, a middle-aged man with a noticeable gut and receding hairline seems to be playing a game on his laptop.

Ten feet past him, in front of the last window, in the opposite corner of the room, is a guy about my age. He has a dark complexion with curly brown hair that falls just below his ears. He has headphones in and is slowly bobbing his head to whatever beat is bumping through them. He is scribbling intently into a notebook and biting on his lower lip, deep in concentration.

Working on a college paper? But handwriting it? Interesting.

I try not to stare but I can't seem to pull my gaze away from him. He reminds me of someone. Not my brothers, not Derek, but someone from my past life.

But who?

Avenged Innocence

He must have felt my gaze on him because he looks up and his eyes meet mine. His lips curl into a sexy half-smile and it clicks.

Levi. Levi Prather.

That's who he reminds me of.

I slouch down into my chair and start mindlessly scrolling through the Edmonson's friends' feeds to see if anymore tidbits jump out at me, but my concentration is broken.

I sneak another peek at the Levi-Look-Alike. He's back to furiously putting pen to paper.

The resemblance is uncanny.

It can't be him. Can it? If it is, he didn't seem to recognize me. As much as I need that to be a relief, it hurts a little.

Knock it off, Christina. It's probably not him and even if it were, it's been six years.

The memory flashes through my mind like snapshots.

It had been about two years since Derek moved; and about a year and half since *it* happened.

Levi was in my grade and we had been acquaintances for a while. (My friends were his friends type of deal.) There were four girls in our group (I called them 'my girls') Chelly, Tara, Grace and me. We had been friends since kindergarten. When we were in eighth grade, Grace started 'dating' Cole. He was Levi's best friend. Since 'dating' consisted of merely standing by each other in a crowd, Levi and I hung out by default.

When there was a dance, Levi asked his friend Mike to ask my friend Chelly, to ask me if I would go with him.

I said no.

Chelly, a freckled face imp of a girl with a button nose and chipmunk cheeks (one of those girls who will be cute her whole life) protested. I can still hear her doll-like voice in my head.

"Aurora, you've been weird lately. If it's about Derek you have got to let it go. He's gone. He moved away. He's not coming back. You don't talk to

anyone anymore. You barely smile. You always look like you're mad or thinking too hard. You're so serious. You need to have fun. Lighten up."

I listened to her. I heard every word she said. But my own script was running through the back of my mind.

"You have no idea, Chelly. No idea. I am always thinking. I have my own personal horror film playing on repeat through my mind at all times. If the instance wasn't enough, if that alone wouldn't have wrecked my childhood, there was also what took place immediately after... Unimaginable until it actually happened. Then every possible emotion a twelve-year-old girl can have was magnified a thousand percent and crammed into a ten-minute window. That ten minutes has dominated my life ever since."

But of course I couldn't say any of that. So I just let her talk. I had my resolute 'no' ready to go again until she finished with, "Maybe we should talk to Mrs. Henry." The guidance counselor.
"Ok, ok, I'll go." And I forced a smile.
"Yay!" She actually jumped and clapped her hands together like a toddler. Emphasizing her childlike appearance.
That Saturday night, mom drove me to Chelly's house where there were four couples meeting for pictures before the dance.
'My girls' (Chelly, Tara, and Grace) were all done up the nines. They looked gorgeous. Fancy hair. Makeup done perfectly.
I looked alright.
By this time, mom and I were almost the same size so she helped me find one of her simple black dresses and matching high heels. She curled my hair but I had refused makeup. I would rather look plain than look like a clown.
Levi looked gorgeous. Stunning. He could have walked right out of a magazine.
Like library Levi, real-life Levi had dark brown curls that looped up just below his ears. He was wearing dark blue jeans, a black polo, and black loafers. The other guys were in suits. I was happy Levi wasn't.

Avenged Innocence

The photo shoot was an awkward arrangement of boys on one side and girls on the other. No one knew how to act. The girls messed with their hair. The boys picked on each other.

Then when Chelly's mom asked everyone to couple up, no one knew how they should stand or what they should do with their hands. It resulted in a lot of giggling. After the mothers were satisfied that the night was sufficiently captured on film, they let us leave. But not before giving hugs and kisses all around.

Chelly lived a couple blocks from our school so we walked to the dance, after separating back into boys and girls. I let myself enjoy the silliness of being in a goofy gaggle of girls.

I had grown up quickly after losing my dad in second grade but I changed even more after *it* happened when I was in sixth grade. There hadn't been much joy or laughing since then. I guess the timing was a blessing to some extent. Twelve year old girls tend to be moody anyway. No one said anything when my behavior became erratic. I'm lucky to have friends and family who loved me through it all.

I really wish that would've been enough.

The dance was fun. Our theme was 'A Night Under the Stars'. Pretty original. The gym was decorated with lots of black balloons and cheap decorations. There was a table set up with punch, pretzels, crackers and other snacks for the hormone-riddled teens to nervously munch on. The playlist started with a lot of upbeat music. The eight of us stayed together in a back corner. We rocked out to the YMCA, Thriller, and The Macarena. Oldies but goodies.

When Aerosmith sang 'I Don't Want to Miss a Thing', we swayed together in a large circle and belted out the lyrics using our closed fists as microphones.

For almost an hour I had completely forgotten about *the instance* and my dad.

For the first time in over two years I was happy.

Then the opening words to 'I Swear' filled the gymnasium.

The couples sheepishly paired off.

Levi turned toward me and shyly extended his hand. I took it and felt an unfamiliar wiggling in my stomach. I couldn't discern if it was a good feeling or not until he slipped his hands over my hips.

My heart soared and I looked into his eyes for the first time. He was still holding me at arm's length but he bent his elbows slightly and pulled me in a little closer. It was a good feeling. Definitely a good feeling.

We moved together, back and forth, and he pulled me in even tighter.

He looped his left arm all the way around my back and took my right hand in his. There we were in the dimly lit gymnasium. Swaying together, our bodies touching, our interlaced fingers resting near my chin on his chest.

My stomach was swarming with butterflies.

My breath was short and excited.

My heart was a bass drum.

I could see in his eyes he wanted to kiss me.

That's when a switch flipped inside of me.

My mind, my heart, my body… everything changed.

When Levi leaned in to kiss me, something happened. The only way I can describe it would be that a primitive flight or fight instinct took over and my body wanted to fight.

I felt his breath on my face, his hand slowly rubbing my lower back, his sweaty palm on mine and I couldn't stop myself. My hand crushed his, my knee automatically jerked up, aiming for his most tender area. Luckily my mind gained control before contact was made. I shifted from fight to flight.

I turned and left.

No goodbyes. No explanations. I had to get out of there.

I needed some air.

I managed to keep my pace at a walk until I was out the door. As soon as the night air hit my face, I kicked off my mom's shoes, grabbed one in each hand and broke into a sprint. I ran until all the physical urges in my body were drained.

Avenged Innocence

My lungs were heaving for air and my legs felt like mush.

I didn't have a cell phone and I didn't have any money. I walked home. It was only a couple miles and I had already run halfway there.

I used the rest of that walk to think.

I knew then, in that moment, what I had suspected for a while.

I had to leave.

I started to plan my exit strategy.

I had to run away.

I needed a new ID with a cell phone and debit card associated with it.

I also knew I needed another transaction.

I had been trying to decipher the emotions from that afternoon. The afternoon *it* happened.

But now I knew.

I needed it again.

It controlled my thoughts anyway.

The most awful experience to happen to me physically had been followed by the most invigorating high.

And I had been craving it ever since.

Thinking about *it* brings me back to the task at hand; Paul.

(I can't call him Richie. Can't do it.)

I glance at the time.

Three-ten. Finally.

I turn my back to the Levi-Look-Alike and concentrate on my phone. I open up PlayRound and see there's another envelope added to my mail, making it four messages to manage.

I click on Paul's first. A generic 'hope you had a good day. math was super hard. had a test'.

Just a keep-in-touch message to make sure his little friend stays in contact.

Gross.

My face twists in disgust as I reply, 'great day. dodgeball in PE. im sure you did good on your test! ;)'.

Elle Iverson

The chicken's message says, 'hi'.
I reply back in kind.
The new one is a brown dog with his tongue sticking out.
His message says, 'how old r u?'
Hmmm… either a kid or a stupid pervert. I'll let the cops figure out which. I delete the message without replying.

Finally, I click the envelope from the blue bunny sporting the headphones and sunglasses.

As I read the words, my blood runs cold.

'I know who you are.
I know what you did.'

CHAPTER 12

My mind is reeling.

I close the app, shut my phone completely off, and shove it to the bottom of Pac. I grab my charger and do a quick sweep of the area to make sure I'm not leaving anything behind and also to see if anyone is watching me.

I grab Pac and dart to the bathroom.

I try to walk nonchalantly and I'm relieved when I burst into the bathroom and discover it's empty. I drop Pac next to me and splash water on my face. Cold, prickly water. It stings and takes my breath away.

Who?

How?

Who?!

Why?!?

Who?!?!

All the questions.

Two things are possible:

#1. Someone who knows me as Christina has figured out that I am Darcy on the app.

#2. Someone has figured out who I really am.

But how?!?!
Who?!?
The first scenario seems unlikely.
But the second seems impossible. I can't bring myself to think of those ramifications. That would ruin everything.
Who?
Who could it be?
And how much do they know?
Do they know I'm a runaway?
Do they know about my addiction?
Who is it?
How much do they know?
And what are they going to do with the info?

I don't know which is worse; if they know who I really am... or if they know what I do as Christina.

CHAPTER 13

I grab Pac and head out of the bathroom and out of the library. I need to leave anyway. I need to get to the business area and find someplace to settle.

The rain has subsided. The luminous gray clouds rolling overhead warn of another storm approaching but I'm going to risk it. I put my head down and walk back in the direction of the BK.

I need to find a home.

I try to distract myself with a game of 'Guess Who's Driving' but one word filters into every thought.

Who?

There's no highway to trudge along this time. It is three miles of stoplights and alternating residential and commercial areas. Too chaotic to zone out.

I try to make a new list:

Library: Check.

Information about Paul: Check.

Now I'm onto the third task: Finding a home.

What should I do tomorrow?

I think I should venture back to Paul's to see what I can see.

My mind is refusing to acknowledge the overriding thought that threatens to ruin everything.

In response, I start mumbling the lyrics to Destiny's Child 'Survivor' in a subconscious attempt to ward off the fear.

I watch the cars passing by and peer into each one. But instead of playing my game, I find myself wondering, 'Are you Blue Bunny?'

The time passes quickly and before I know it, I see the BK sign from this morning.

I stop to get my bearings. Mentally pushing all the questions and creeping anxiety away. I need to focus on survival now. The interstate is to my left. The BK is straight ahead and the factory area is to my right. I decide to try my hand at the interstate exit ramp.

When I walk underneath the overpass, I see two figures hiding up at the very top in the same nook area where I changed my clothes last night. They appear to be children.

There is one person down at the light holding a sign. She's a middle-aged black woman with an afro divided into two equal puffs on the sides of her head. She has a large cardboard box sitting at her feet.

Her sign reads, 'Homeless and hungry. Anything Helps. God Bless.'

Although she doesn't seem to have missed many meals. She's not fat, but the crop top she's wearing reveals a round midsection. And the black yoga pants she has on leave little to the imagination.

Baby got back.

Sir Mix-A-Lot's lyrics bounce through my thoughts as I watch her walk to a car where an elderly gentleman is holding a bill out the window. She takes it and I hear her thank him.

When she turns to resume her post, she sees me. Her first reaction is to glare. I guess I have that effect on people.

"Can I help you?" She asks with a lot of attitude.

"I'm not looking to take your spot. My name is Christina. I'm new here. Is there a group nearby?"

The light changes to green and the cars move passed us.

Avenged Innocence

She looks at me skeptically. I see her sizing me up from top to bottom. She starts with my tight white shirt all the way down to my dirty shoes. Then she eyes Pac. I notice her take a long look at both of my arms, probably looking for track marks.

"How long you been on the street?"

"Four years."

"Where are you from?"

"Minnesota."

The last answer causes her to raise an eyebrow and I know she has a follow-up question but the light changes back to red, bringing a whole new wave of customers to her storefront.

I shut up and back away. She slowly makes her walk up the row of cars. A few windows roll down and hands emerge holding cash, food, or bags. The bags are a somewhat new concept. They're called blessing bags and they're a great option for good samaritans who want to help but are afraid homeless people will blow cash on … well, blow and booze.

I stay silent as she makes her way up and down the row of cars, taking the handouts and thanking each person.

Then she walks back to me as the light changes and the cars begin to move.

"Minnesota, huh? Why you here now?"

"The winters are terrible up there…I'd freeze to death by November."

I can't tell if she believes me. But again, it's not a lie. It's just not the full truth.

"How old are you?" She's allowed to vet me. To ask questions and feel me out.

But it would be rude for me to reciprocate.

"Nineteen."

"You ran away?"

I nod.

"Your daddy rape you?"

I shake my head. "No. He died."

"And your mama?"

I let my gaze match hers. My expression remains unchanged. Sometimes the best thing to say is nothing.

The light changes back to red.

Our eyes stay locked until she finally says, "I gotta 'nother hour or so here. Head up 'der with the boys. Keep quiet. I'll be there to fetch ya in bit."

I tuck my chin to my chest and turn to the underpass.

I learned quickly that trust is not easy to come by out here. Especially when you're new. I crawl up to the figures I saw before. They are bigger than I realized. Both teenage boys. One is sleeping with his back to me. The other is curled up, reading a book with a flashlight.

There are a few books sitting out. A couple backpacks leaning against the wall. And each boy has a water bottle sitting next to him.

They've made this concrete patch almost homey.

The boy looks up from his book and watches me as I slide Pac onto the flat surface next to him.

"Who are you?" His tone isn't rude, necessarily, just pointed.

"Christina."

Satisfied, he continues reading his book.

I'm guessing these are her sons.

They look healthy, considering.

Now I wait for her to finish 'working'.

When she's done they'll probably head to wherever they call home.

If I play my cards right, I'll be able to crash with them until this transaction is over.

CHAPTER 14

A crash of thunder startles me awake. It takes me a second to remember where I am, but seeing two poofs of black hair climbing towards us quickly reminds me. I know I didn't sleep well last night but I must have been more tired than I realized to doze off here. It occurs to me that it wasn't thunder that woke me up, but a truck passing on the road overhead.

The woman from the corner is eyeing me as she walks up the forty-five degree angle, balancing the cardboard box in front of her.

She goes to the small space between the reading boy and me, and hoists up the box. Not a subtle hint that she would like me to move over. I do, and she heaves herself next to me.

"Regina. My name is Regina and these here are my boys. Tyrone and Michael."

Tyrone, the reader, offers me a quick two-finger wave without looking up from his book. Michael stirs at the sound of his name.

"How'd your daddy die?"

She's direct, and that's okay, but the mention of my father brings a sharp pain to my chest. The images of the house fire engulfing him float through my mind and I try to push them away.

"He died in a fire." That's the truth. The full truth is that he was a firefighter who was trapped and killed in a house fire that was set intentionally. The police suspected a group of neighborhood kids were the arsonists but there was no evidence and no one was ever charged with the crime. Daddy had died searching the attic for a child who wasn't even there. A baby monitor was found in a back corner. They think someone had been feeding sound through it to make it seem like there was a child in distress. A sicko preying on the devoted firemen who would search... like my dad did. Until the house collapsed around him. He never came out. He died engulfed in flames.

Regina shows no emotion to my answer. She just follows it up with, "You was about to tell me why you ran away from your mama."

She reaches into the box and takes out a plastic bag; it contains two granola bars and two bottles of water. She hands one of each to the boys who both reply with a sincere, "Thank you, Ma'am."

"I'd rather not talk about it, if that's alright."

I could tell by her tense jaw and furrowed brow that it wasn't alright.

"I don't like the idea of some mama bein' worried sick that her baby is out wanderin' the streets or dead in a ditch somewhere."

"She's not worried. I promise." And that is the truth.

I could tell Regina was thinking, weighing the options, figuring out if I am a threat.

I try to sway her by saying, "I'm only passing through. I think I'll be here a few weeks, maybe a month. If you can give me a safe place to sleep then I'll help buy food."

"You'll help?" She raises an eyebrow, curious as to how I plan to pitch in.

"I won't be around during the days, but I'll bring food." She processes this as she digs out an unopened snack-sized bag of pretzels from the box. She tears the top and holds it out to each boy, dumping a few in their hands.

Avenged Innocence

She hesitates for a second before handing the rest of the bag to me.

"Christina, right?"

I nod.

"I have a place you can stay but I have some rules. No boys. No drugs. And you don't tell no one."

I nod again in agreement as I toss the last of the pretzels in my mouth.

Task number three: Check.

Regina takes a couple minutes to sort through the cardboard box. Some people try to be generous on a whim so they'll hand out things they have available. Bottles of water, snacks, even fries they didn't finish from their value meal. Others are prepared with the blessing bags or a little cash on hand. I didn't ask how long Regina had been 'working' today but she had a variety of snacks and a coffee can nearly full of cash. She takes the cash, stacks it up, folds it in half, and jams it in her back pocket. Obviously not trusting to count it in front of me. She empties the food into a backpack next to Michael and shoves her box to the very back, where the concrete slab meets the concrete of the road. In the shadows, it was completely hidden from the street.

We sit in silence for a while. Then, as the sun drops low, Regina stands and heads down to the street. Both boys follow suit and I grab Pac and hurry to keep up.

Michael, who is taller and looks to be a couple years older, carries the backpack containing the food. Tyrone also carries a backpack where he had tossed his book. The four of us head silently toward the factories.

We walk by the massive buildings and the corner where I had spent a restless night the night before. Immediately on the other side of the new commercial area we walk into an old community. It was like stepping through a time warp or into a different dimension. Not even a hundred yards behind us was a bustling culture with stores, restaurants, and businesses all erected in the last twenty years. But here, I stood looking at small houses, most with only one window on the front, barely bigger than the playhouses found in Paul's neighborhood. Most of the houses have bars on that single window and old children's toys piled in the yard. One house in particular looks like a mini-car-junk-yard with a Barbie jeep on three wheels, a little green four-wheeler up on blocks, and a miniature police car with a crunched in bumper.

The lights from businesses and the parking lot flood lights give off enough of a glow for me to barely make all this out. The rest of the houses are sheeted in darkness with only one sad, lonely street light casting a short pitiful glow. Like a bedroom nightlight trying to illuminate a whole house.

My mind starts to race. Do Regina and the boys squat in one of these houses? If so, I would rather take my chances back at the dumpster. Crashing in a vacant house seems like a no-brainer to get off the street but it's actually very dangerous. Sometimes even riskier than sleeping unprotected with the garbage.

For one thing, if you get busted you could go to jail. I can't go to jail. If you go to jail they run fingerprints and try to figure out who you are. Not good.

Secondly, if you're squatting and someone else finds you, you're fair game. Homeowner or other vagabond, both can be deadly.

I haven't crossed that line yet and I don't plan to start now.

But I keep quite. I'll wait and see where they're going.

Regina and the boys move forward. Heads down, minding their own business, walking quickly.

We pass three blocks, I glance down each street and each view is the same as the first. And all are barely visible thanks to the lone hard-working streetlight.

Then there is nothing.

We turn onto a gravel road and it looks like we have been transported a hundred miles away or a hundred years to the past.

I know we are surrounded by developments but there is no evidence of that now except the distant sounds of traffic.

Avenged Innocence

We are in a clearing in the midst of trees. In the middle there stands a small white church next to a cemetery. The few headstones that I can see are crumbling.

As we walk to the church I notice that it also has bars on the windows. Regina walks around to the back. Both boys are playing lookout and watching different directions. I feel like I'm in a spy movie and I would laugh if they weren't so serious.

She slips a key (that I had not seen her produce) into the lock. Then into the deadbolt. She ducks inside and the boys follow. I am right behind them.

No one has spoken since we left the underpass but it is a comfortable quiet between the three of them.

We are standing in, what appears to be, a butler's pantry.

The church is old. The front door probably opens to an auditorium with a large cross hanging on the back wall and we are behind that in an area that looks like it may, at one time, have been a living area for a ground's keeper or parishioner. But now it serves as a storage area. I'm not great at dimensions but I would estimate it at five feet wide and ten feet long with shelves lining both sides. There is barely enough room for us to fit. No one makes an attempt to turn on lights so I try my best to see through the darkness. By the time I close the door behind me and flick both locks, Regina has unlocked another door in the far corner on the opposite wall. She disappears even more into the darkness. The boys follow. When I enter the doorway I am overwhelmed by a wall of thick, strong smell. It is a combination of moth balls and… earth.

I close and lock the door behind me and every internal alarm is flashing in my mind. Screaming for me to freak out. Alerting me that this isn't safe. But there is a warmth between these three that is unmistakable, a shared hurt in all of their eyes that overrides my common sense.

I trace my hand along the wall to guide myself slowly down the rickety steps. I can feel that they're wooden and, the open kind, made with two slim boards.

Regina pulls on a rope light hanging in the middle of the room and I can fully see their home.

I take it all in with a single sweep. It is a dirt cellar (slightly bigger than the room upstairs) with no windows. One wall is lined with the same shelving as the pantry, the other three are bare. The top three shelves are lined with water bottles, canned food, and various other items that were probably collected on a corner.

Everything is organized. In a room this small, it has to be. On the bottom shelf, and stacked on the floor beneath, are books. Probably fifty of them. Stacked neatly in the corner is a pile of blankets. Regina hands two to each of the boys. There are two left. She offers one to me.

"No thanks, you keep them. I have one."

Everyone seems to have their own tiny section.

Regina takes the far right corner, Tyrone sits down directly in front of the shelves, and Michael sits along the wall opposite him. The small spot by the bottom of the stairs was all that remains unclaimed.

I assume that's mine.

I set Pac down and unzip it. I gently remove my blanket. Technically it's more of a thread bare rag than a blanket. The soft satin edges cover three sides; the material is worn from years of being toted around and cuddled. Certain parts are worn all the way through where I rubbed it between my thumb and finger, a tic I have when I am nervous or scared. I lie down and use the blanket to wrap around the upper half of my body. At one time it would have been big enough to cover me from head to toe… but that was before I had to rip it in half. That was a critical piece of my 'beginning a new life' plan.

I suppose it was symbolic, too, in a way. I essentially tore my family apart and used my ripped blanket as the main tool in doing so.

I try to relax my body and turn off my mind. Everything down here is so still. So silent.

Avenged Innocence

But again, the silence doesn't bother me. I'm used to it... but it is peculiar. There's a definite love and respect shared among these three. It's as if they communicate everything simply with looks and feelings. No words need to be exchanged. It's almost as if they're afraid to say anything out loud... like verbalizing the cause of their underlying sadness will make it true.

I wonder what their story is.

I usually enjoy speculating but something about Regina makes it hard to get a read on her. Her demeanor suggests that she has built walls so high and impenetrable that nothing and no one will get through. Except the boys. She's built her walls to surround them too.

Regina pulls on a large t-shirt and oversized sweats to cover her original revealing outfit.

Everyone settles into their blanket beds and I feel Michael looking at me.

"Where you from?" He nods his head up as he asks with a surprisingly deep voice.

He's a lean boy but the voice is a low, like the rumble from train tracks.

Before I have a chance to answer, Regina cuts in with, "Michael."

Her tone is sharp but not harsh. The boy lowers his head, inhales through his nose and slowly exhales through his mouth.

"Sorry Mama..." Then he raises his head back in my direction and continues, "May I ask where you are from?" His tone is not mocking or sarcastic. It's respectful and inquiring.

"Minnesota." I smile, pulling my legs up to my chest and leaning against Pac.

"May I ask how old you are?"

"Nineteen."

"I'm sixteen."

He seems older.

Regina pipes up again from her pallet, "That's enough Michael. Get back to your studies."

Obediently he opens his book and slides out a pen and paper from the backpack Tyrone had been carrying. That's when I notice which book he is reading. Advanced Algebra. He turns to a new page in the notebook and starts writing letters and numbers and working equations without a calculator.

I glance at Tyron's book. *The Complete History of the United States of America 1776 to Today.*

This is a first.

Regina has also settled back with a book but the cover is plain green with a black binding, I can't tell what it is. The single swinging light bulb is casting as many shadows as it is illuminating pages.

My eyes skim over the titles of the other books still on the shelf behind Tyrone. Not what I would expect in a teenage boy's library. A variety of history, math, and science books. Along with great classics like *Moby Dick and The Adventures of Tom Sawyer.*

"May I?"

Regina nods, "Of course."

I select *To Kill a Mockingbird* and sit back to relax for the first time in… I don't even know how long.

I've stayed with different groups before. Setting up camps in alleys, under bridges, and once in an abandoned mall, but there was always a sense of paranoia. I never let my guard down. But something about this family makes me feel safe. Maybe part of it is knowing we are sleeping under a worship sanctuary. Maybe it is feeling like we are in a setting that takes place before the era of social media and online terrors. Whatever it is, I doze off while reading about Scout and Boo Radley and I sleep as soundly as if I am in my old room, decked out in purple paint with posters tacked up on the walls and Taylor Swift playing on the radio.

CHAPTER 15

I wake up to Regina and the boys laughing and thunder booming.

There is an amazing aroma filling the small space. Coffee.

I open my eyes and wipe away the spittle that had run onto my cheek. I guess it's been awhile since I slept so soundly.

"Good morning." Regina greets me warmly and offers me a small plastic cup with steam curling from the lid.

"The gas station down the way has a special this month; buy two donuts get a coffee free. These two get the donuts, we get the coffees."

"Sounds like a good deal to me." And I mean it.

"You look like a two cream, two sugars girl." She was right.

I take a sip and it is heaven. Perfection.

I tell Regina as much and her response is to stand and say, "Ok, well, enjoy it. We're hunkering down here all day. It's Sunday. The Lord's day."

And that's what we do. All day. We hunker down. We read, sleep, and snack on the reserves. There is minimal conversation but it's comforting, not uncomfortable.

I am able to turn off my mind and enjoy reading about the old time pace of Alabama during the depression through the classic writing style of Harper Lee. I never would have imagined I would read for fun, but this particular novel had been an assignment the year I left. Unfortunately, I disappeared before I finished it. This is a time capsule for me in a few different ways; reading about life during the Great Depression and remembering my life before *The Instance*. It is relaxing.

In fact, I find myself dozing off and on. I spend some time in that unfamiliar space of not-sleeping but not-awake. Memories play through my thoughts like dreams.

The thunder claps.

The image of 'my girls' and me at Tara's house the first year we became friends flits across my eyelids. We were all in the same kindergarten class and Tara's mom, being the room mom, wanted to get to know the other families. She invited us over for Sunday dinner. The best part, the part that holds a special place in my heart, was that their yellow lab, Dolly, had recently given birth to a litter of wiggly, squirmy, soft puppies. The kids sat on the floor and let them pummel us. I will never forget the smell of puppy kisses. It's unlike anything else. The feeling of their soft fur as it brushed against my face. Their little paws batting at our hands, their sharp little teeth grabbing onto our socks. My friends and I giggling as our parents circled around us, corralling the puppies and laughing at the perfect scene.

It was one of my favorite memories. It used to fill my heart with pure joy. I was literally surrounded by everyone I loved and playing with puppies. It was every six year-old's dream. It used to be a go-to thought when I needed to cheer up.

Not anymore. Now it's tainted. Now puppy dreams will never bring anything but sorrow. It never fails; whenever I see a puppy, my next thought is of Conrad. Then Conrad with a puppy.

Then Clearing Boy... Then my daddy... My mind snaps shut.

It is a spiral of flashbacks that only brings me pain. My subconscious spares me anymore memories and I slip off to dreamland where visions of Paul replace any unpleasant thoughts.

The next morning the same coffee conversation takes place but when I say, "Thank you." Regina responds with, "Well enjoy it 'cause we gotta get goin.'"

Avenged Innocence

And just like that, everyone stands to tidy their area. Blankets are folded, books re-shelved, and the small space is just as we had entered a few nights ago.

We head up the stairs.

We step into the morning that is already warming with the sun.

"Walk with me?" Regina asks but it isn't really a question.

I hoist Pac onto my back and step quickly to catch up with her but while I am still a pace behind she says, "I wasn't kidding. The rules apply. You seem like a nice girl, Christina. I want to help you but those boys are my life. You can stay here for a bit, heck I hope we're only here for a little while longer, but you can't tell anyone. You can never come here during the daylight, and if I so much as suspect that you're doing drugs, or have drugs on you, well..."

She lets the threat trail off but she stares back at me before finishing with, "Understood?"

"Yes ma'am."

"We'll see you tonight between six and seven. If you're late don't bother comin. You come and go with us or you don't come and go at all."

She stops abruptly, turns, and wraps me in a hug. My entire body goes stiff as a board.

"You're too young to be so jaded." She whispers and then drops her arms to her sides and leads the boys toward their station.

I turn and head towards Aspen Views.

It's still early so I have plenty of time to walk, plus I need time to plan out my day.

Today is Monday, which means Gretchen will take the girls to story time at the library.

I need to get into their house. Paul doesn't take a bus or train so if his car's gone, he's gone. Same with Gretchen. And one nice thing about Gretchen staying home with the girls is that I don't need to worry about a nanny-cam.

Elle Iverson

I decide to play it by ear. I'll see what feels right when I get there. Until then, I'm going to play 'Guess Who's Driving'. I watch the cars tick by on the highway, though the only life I'm curious about at the moment is Regina's. That's a story I want to know but I'm afraid to ask. She seems street smart but also out of place. For as strict as she is with her boys (and as intent as she is on me pulling my own weight) why aren't they helping? Why aren't they taking a turn in the hot sun instead of holed-up reading under the underpass?

How long have they been living on the street? And why?

These are a few of the questions I want to ask but can't. Not yet anyway. Right now I'm thankful for the food and shelter. Which reminds me; I need to find some food. That was my end of the deal. I'll add that to the to-do list for today.

I see a black car heading toward me. It could be a Maxima. My heart leaps and my mind races. Why didn't I think of that? This is the only main road linking the subdivision to anything. Of course this is the way Paul would drive to work. It's not the end of the world if he sees me, he's not gonna recognize me from the playground a couple days ago, but it's still better to not be seen. Not to draw any attention to myself.

My eyes dart around. There is a gas station about half a mile ahead. I duck in to regroup. It's small. An off-brand four-pump operation. I like the bigger truck stops because I'm able to slip in and out undetected. This door chimes as I walk in and the gentleman behind the counter looks up from his magazine and greets me with a 'Good morning' but his eyes don't convey the same sentiment. I dodge into the bathroom.

Notice a theme developing?

I can't say I ever dreamed that one day I would find such solace in bathrooms, or so eagerly seek them out in gas stations and fast food establishments, but bathrooms are literally the only place I can get any sort of privacy or do any personal grooming. This lovely commode is dingy and dirty. I eye a spot on the floor

Avenged Innocence

that is either a bug or stain. Either way, it hurries me to go about my business.

I brush my teeth and use the hand soap to lather up my white shirt after switching back into my black tank. I use the sink to wash all my 'laundry' from my baggies. I wring them out as best I can. Then I fish my phone out of the bottom of Pac and quickly put everything else away except my clothes. I use my homeless shirt to bundle up my damp clothes and hold it like a baby on my hip.

I head out of the bathroom, buy a Clif bar from the still-skeptical clerk, and return outside.

The sun is fully out and it's starting to get warm. There are parking stalls all the way around the small gas station but, for the few minutes I've been here, there haven't been any other customers.

I decide to hang out in the back until most of the traffic (including Paul) has passed.

In the corner, and off to the side, there is a dumpster that is surrounded by a rickety wooden fence (presumably to keep critters at bay). This is a great spot to dry my clothes. I hang them on the back of the fence, one item on each plank, out of sight to anyone driving by. The fence isn't very long but, luckily, I don't have very many clothes.

I sit down on the curb and turn on my phone.

A fresh wave of anxiety washes over me and I remember the Blue Bunny message from a couple days ago. I had completely blocked it out. But now it comes rushing back.

The stress.

The questions.

The dread.

I have to see if he's messaged again. I hurriedly open the app and, no surprise, three messages. I ignore Paul and Chicken (it's school hours anyway) and I tap the sunglasses-wearing bunny.

"No response? C'mon Christina. You're better than that."

Ok. Well, that's one question answered.

I close out of the app without responding.

He 'knows' I'm Christina.

But who is it and how did he find me?

I try to retrace my steps from the past month. Who did I introduce myself to? When did I use my 'real' name? And then, how did that person track me down on the app? What do they want?

Should I disappear? Forget about Paul and just get the heck out of here?

But what if Blue Bunny is watching me?

Where will I go?

And with what money?

Once again; so many questions.

And no way to get answers.

At least not on this topic.

I switch my focus back to Paul.

Traffic has slowed down. Anyone going to work in the city would need to be past here by now. It should be perfect timing to get into position before Gretchen heads out. I want to see what time she leaves so I can gauge when she'll be back.

My clothes are still damp... do I risk leaving them here or deal with trying to dry them out later?

I think they'll be fine.

I grab Pac and head to the giant stone that marks the entrance to Aspen Views.

CHAPTER 16

I don't go directly to Paul and Gretchen's house. I remember the for-sale sign in one of the yards behind theirs. I quickly circle back and, sure enough, it's still there. And there are no cars in the driveway. That, and the overgrown lawn, is good sign. I peer into the backyard and see a raised playset, a little house that looks like it was built on stilts. There are swings on one side and a slide on the other. The structure sits roughly five feet off the ground and is kitty-corner from Paul's backyard.

I slide my phone out of my back pocket and punch in the number listed below the 'See Me' invitation printed on the sign.

"Adam's Reality. Kirsten speaking." A pleasant, very receptionisty voice chirps.

"Hello. My name is Betty and I'm interested in seeing the listing on Poplar Lane."

"Wonderful, let me connect you with that agent."

"Thank you."

The hold music is set to a radio station and FGL serenades me with 'Cruise' while I wait.

The house next door, directly behind Paul and Gretchen's, has a privacy fence. But the one I'm inquiring about (and the one I'll be watching) don't.

I'm humming along with the catchy chorus when a deep voice comes on the line.

"This is Jack."

"Hi Jack, my name is Betty. I'm calling about the listing on Poplar Lane."

"Sure Betty. Well, it's a great house. Great location. Great schools. Very reasonable asking price. It's a four bedroom, three bath, with a bonus room."

"Yes, I saw it online and love it. We would actually like to come take a look…"

"Oh absolutely. When did you have in mind?"

"My husband should be off work around five…"

It's quiet on the other end of the line and I can hear him shuffling papers around. Maybe he actually keeps an old-fashioned desk calendar. Or he's trying to find his cell phone for his google calendar; that's more likely.

He must've found whichever he was looking for because he says, "It looks like five o'clock tonight will work great."

"Oh shoot. I forgot my daughter has soccer practice. How about seven?"

"That should be fine." He says it hesitantly. He's probably seeing how he can rework his night to make it 'fine'.

"Dang it. I just remembered a PTA meeting I have to be at… would eight be too late?"

"Ummm, no. That should be fine." He sounds even less enthused. "But the family has already relocated so the house is empty if tomorrow will work better for you."

Ding.

"Ok, let's do this. I'll call and get my husband's schedule figured out, get these crazy kids' schedules down, and I'll call you back with a set time."

"Sounds great. Can I get your contact info before you go?"

"I left it with Kirsten. Talk soon." I hang up before he realizes that I hadn't left any info with Kirsten. In fact, I had *67 before dialing so it'll show up as 'Private' on their caller ID.

But now I know the house is empty.

Avenged Innocence

I'm not planning on going inside. As I mentioned earlier, vacant houses are dangerous and ones that are for sale, especially in this type of neighborhood, are harder to break into than prison is to break out of.

No, I won't be going in but the playset in the backyard will work wonderfully for a stakeout area. It's not as glamorous as a maintenance van but it'll be more than enough for me.

It's a nice playset. It's pretty big and it looks fairly new. The features I'm most interested in are the little windows. They have shutters that open and close, providing privacy. Without hesitating, I walk quickly over to the structure, throw Pac inside, and climb the ladder.

I pull the shutters closed, except the one facing Paul's house, and peer around to see if anyone noticed me.

There's no movement in the quiet neighborhood.

Thanks to large windows and a glass sliding back door, I can see straight into Paul and Gretchen's kitchen. There is a bedroom window to one side and it looks like another bedroom window above it.

I recognize Gretchen from her Facebook profile. She's cutting up fruit onto plates for the girls who are both seated at an island. She looks a little heavier in real life than online but she's still very pretty.

I check my phone again.

Nine forty-five.

They should be leaving for story time soon. I'll make myself at home here until then.

I watch Gretchen dote on her children. She's obviously in love with them; smiling, laughing, tending to their every whim. The girls, in turn, are totally reliant on her. Even from here I can sense the connection. The bond between a mother and her child is unlike any other.

My heart falls a little as I realize I'll probably never experience it. Not from the parental perspective anyway. Part of me is sad I'll never have kids. There is also a part of me that's sad that these precious girls' happy little lives are about to be rocked to the core. In an instant, everything will change. They will have to adjust to growing up without a daddy.

Their life may be harder at first, but the world will be a better place for it in the end. Men like Paul, who prey on young boys and girls, who have a sickness that there is no cure for; the world is better off without them.

I suppose I have a sickness too.

But at least I'm trying to use mine for good. Even at the expense of not being able to live a normal life.

The 'experts' say that people like me aren't supposed to feel love or empathy.

They say we don't have a conscience.

But that's not true.

At least not for me.

I love. I love deeply. I love my mom and I love my brothers. I loved my daddy. I love Derek. I already care about Regina and the boys.

I can be empathetic. I can be empathetic to Gretchen and her girls and what they are about to go through. I can be empathetic to women who have been abused.

I can be empathetic.

I care.

I love.

I'm just damaged.

I can pinpoint the exact minute I became broken or (back to my inner quandary) the exact minute I realized I was broken.

I think about that day all the time.

It haunts me.

And it fuels me.

CHAPTER 17

Every detail from the day *the instance* occurred is etched in my memory and I can replay it like a movie.

I was twelve years old.

Daddy had been gone for four years.

I was at the park with my brothers. Mom had warned us about the dangers of talking to strangers; but he wasn't a stranger. He was a boy in William's grade. I didn't know him. (I still can't remember his name. He'll forever be Clearing Boy to me.) He had always been nice to me and polite around my parents. That day, I was walking to the slide when he told me there was a litter of kittens that the mama cat had hidden under a log and asked if I wanted to see them.

Of course I did. He was cute and who doesn't love kittens?

We walked a ways into the woods. I think I knew something was off but I would have never imagined what was actually about to happen.

We veered off the path through the brush. It was thick. I was wearing a pink spring dress with white daisies printed along the bottom. I remember the branches scratching my arms and the thorns cutting my legs. I remember the clouds shading the sun. The treetops getting so thick that there was barely any light peeking through. Then we stepped into a small clearing,

Elle Iverson

completely covered in shade, and the clouds eclipsed the sun, and it was pitch black. Just for a second.

That's when he grabbed me.

The nice, quiet boy who I had a crush on, spun me around, looped his arm between both of my elbows, and grabbed my hair.

"Not a word." He hissed in my ear. His spittle landing on my cheek and neck.

Then he let go of my arms but used my hair to force me to my knees. He crouched down behind me, using his free hand to lift up my skirt and pull down my Hello Kitty panties. Still holding my hair, he pushed me to the ground. My body landed hard but my head snapped back because of his grip on my hair. My neck was craning up and my head was inches away from a large rock. Then my face crashed into the hard earth as his body landed on top of mine, knocking the air out of my lungs and pushing my cheek further into the dirt.

Grass, leaves, and soil covered my face. I breathed in the damp taste of it all; choking as it clogged my nostrils. My tears mixed with the dirt, caking my face with mud.

I could feel him on top of me. His weight heavy on my back as he positioned himself. He used his legs to force mine open but my panties were caught around my knees, making it difficult.

But not impossible.

I hear screaming in my head but my voice comes out as only a whimpering plea, "Please stop. Please don't. Please."

But seconds later, a burst of pain erupts as he enters me.

His breath is hot on my neck.

I feel him rocking on top of me.

His hands on my back, digging into my shoulders.

I stare at the rock in front of my face and start counting.

Pretending I am anywhere but here.

I realize I am counting to the rhythm of his movements.

17 back, 18 forward, 19 back, 20 forward.

I feel his release at 87.

Avenged Innocence

Then he collapsed on top of me, bringing his hand around my throat and his mouth to my ear.

"Tell anyone about this, anyone, and I'll kill your mommy... just like the fire that I set killed your daddy."

Time stopped. The pain in my back, the sores on my arms, the cuts on my legs, my tears, my sobs, the ache of my lost innocence – they were all replaced with white hot anger.

There was no more pain. Just an all-consuming need to hurt him.

He had set the fire.

It had been neighborhood kids.

Without thinking, I ducked my chin all the way to my chest and brought my head up as hard as I could. It connected with his nose. I heard a satisfying 'crack'. His hands instinctively went to his face and he rolled to the side. I felt warm droplets of blood between my shoulder blades as I used my arms to push myself up on all fours.

He was lying on his side on the ground next to me with blood dripping through his fingers as he cradled his nose. His eyes flashed with anger; but it was unparalleled to mine. I grabbed the rock that had served as my focal point and jumped on top of him, rolled him onto his back and slammed the rock into his ear as hard as I could

He wasn't expecting it and the force made him disoriented. Not unconscious but confused.

I used my legs (like he had done) as a brace on top of his. My feet locked on the inside of his hips, both of my hands around his throat.

I used every ounce of pressure I had to balance on his throat and thighs. His arms flailed around. His hands slapped my face, pulled my hair, grabbed at my fingers. He was trying his best to knock me off. But I didn't feel any of it. I just watched his eyes. Wide and bulging. Tears pouring out of them.

I was using all my weight but he was still breathing. I realized my palms were pressing into his collarbone, not on his windpipe so I made a small adjustment.

My brothers and I used to play a game where two people sit at opposite ends of a table and one person would flick a piece of paper (folded into the shape of a football) through the other person's hands that were in the shape of a goal post (both thumbs touching and pointer-fingers extended). That's how I adjusted my hands, but instead of having my thumbs touching, I put them side by side. With that little tweak, my hands were no longer wrapped around his neck, but more efficiently, the upside down goal post was crushing his esophagus. I could feel his throat collapsing.

I stared into his eyes. Moments ago they portrayed an innocent kid. Then evil desires.

But now all I saw was terror.

His arms fell feebly to his sides. His hands were still loosely pulling on my fingers.

Then his legs went limp.

I watched his eyes roll back.

I felt his chest beneath me stop moving.

His eyes, completely empty, stared off behind me.

I just sat there.

To say I was overwhelmed by emotions is an understatement.

I experienced every possible emotion at once.

And I experienced them all in droves.

Like waves of colors crashing over me.

Blue fear from the attack.

Red anger from learning he was the reason my dad was gone.

Green adrenaline coursing through my veins.

And also a yellow euphoria that I had never known before. A freeing sense that seemed to open up my chest and let my heart soar.

Avenged Innocence

The last moment when I watched the light in his eyes flicker and then the portal to his soul finally burn out, something ignited in me.

Having that barrage of emotions at one time, at such a young age, and with so much intensity... it crossed wires in my mind.

At the dance with Levi, I had an inkling of the yellow feeling beginning to fester and I instantly craved more. The only way my mind knew how to get there was to look for the light... and put it out.

That's why I had to leave.

Not just the dance; but leave my life.

I had thought about it every day (almost all day) since.

When Chelly had been lecturing me, that's what had been running through my mind.

I knew I wouldn't hurt Levi but I also knew that I needed to experience the waves of colors again.

I needed to feel the power, the control, the happiness; I needed to feel the whole rainbow. Bits and pieces were illuminated during different events but nothing opened my eyes and drenched me with the feelings so intensely as what had happened in the clearing.

On the walk home from the dance that night I had started planning my exit strategy. I couldn't simply run away. I couldn't just disappear. Mom would search for me. So I devised a plan. It seemed genius at the time, and I suppose it was to a point, because it worked. I'm here. Getting to experience the high of all highs while simultaneously ridding the world of creeps like Paul.

Yes, I feel deeply.

I love strongly.

I just happen to have an addiction to killing people.

CHAPTER 18

I'm crouching on my knees in the tiny treehouse to get a perfect view of Paul's kitchen. I stretch my legs one at a time and roll my eyes when my knees pop. With the chorus of aches and pains you would think I was on my way into a nursing home instead of knocking on the door of twenty years old.
I watch Gretchen wipe both girls' faces. She kisses the tops of their heads as she lifts them down from their highchairs. Speaking softly to them as she lovingly guides them to the front door. She stoops down and I watch her slip shoes on the girls, grab a large diaper bag, and a thermos of coffee and they head out the door.

I listen closely. I hear a van door slide shut. I hear another door close. Then the engine fires up and fades away.

Here we go. I grab Pac to pull it on my shoulders, but then I pause. I gotta be quick. I haven't seen anyone else the whole time I've been waiting here. The chances of someone coming to the tree house, seeing Pac, and taking it are slim. It would be much easier to leave it here rather than hauling it inside.

Nope, I can't do it.

I slip Pac on and shimmy down the stairs. I quickly cross the adjoining lawns and walk deliberately to the sliding glass back door connected to the kitchen. It attracts less attention when you're purposeful. Slinking is suspicious. I walk intentionally through the back door.

Avenged Innocence

It may surprise you (or it may not) to know that most people leave back doors completely unlocked and alarms unarmed during the day. Front doors may get locked but back doors and patio sliders are usually not given a second thought.

I step into the kitchen and it's refreshingly cool. I didn't realize how warm it was outside until I was greeted by a rush of cold air upon entering the house.

The air conditioning feels amazing but the smell of warm cinnamon drifting through the house is what is really inviting. Even though I wasn't invited. In fact, I'm probably unwanted, but I don't let that detour me. I make my way into the open concept kitchen, living room, and dining room area. The kitchen is spacious with a large black granite island, white cabinets, and stainless steel appliances. The whole space has a modern feel to it. My first stop is under the sink. I find the garbage bags and I take one. I don't know what I'm looking for but one of the lessons I've learned is that it's nice to have the option handy to take things with me.

Usually I don't find much but every once in a while something interesting presents itself.

Paul's house is neat but 'lived-in'. There are a few dishes in the sink and a handful of pink and purple toys strewn about the living room.

I walk through the main area, past a gray sectional, and a large television mounted on the wall. The master bedroom is straight ahead, I can see the king-sized bed through the open door. The giant bed is positioned so the white headboard is centered in the room. It's also modern-themed. The only other furniture are two white night tables positioned on either side of the bed.

Minimalistic. Clean.

I walk to the side table closest to the door and open the drawer. There are a few pieces of crumpled up paper, some pens, cough drops, and toenail clippers. This must be Paul's.

I go to the other side. On the top of this table is a book on parenting stacked underneath a bible. This must be Gretchen's.

Her drawer has lotion, chap-stick, and a nail file. Nothing of real interest.

I walk through the giant master bathroom back to the closet. It is very organized and it's separated into his and hers. 40/60 respectively.

There are hanging sections and open shelving. I suppose this design is convenient so people can see their wardrobe at a glance instead of going through the trouble of opening drawers.

I chose to simplify it even more by not having a wardrobe. If I'm wearing one outfit, I know I have exactly two other outfits to choose from. I am nothing if not efficient.

I thumb through Gretchen's belongings first, out of curiosity more than agenda. She has a nice style; Casual chic, I think it's called.

There is a large mahogany jewelry box nestled in the corner. I open the top and it's a glittering layer of earrings. Some diamonds, some sapphires, one set of pearls, and a lot of sterling silver. I let myself admire it for just one moment before closing the lid and moving on to Paul's side.

His style is pretty basic.

Shirts, suits, and ties. Half dozen dress shoes and a couple loafers. I also see one pair of running shoes, they're fairly unworn.

I'm trying to figure out if Paul is in good shape. The lack of a gym bag, no weights at home, and no workout clothes are indicators that he probably isn't trying to buff up.

I leave the bedroom and cross back through the living area where there are two more doors. Both are open. One is a bathroom. Well, there's no bath, just a toilet and sink... does that make it a powder room? Regardless, it's clean and smells like lemons.

The other open door leads to an office.

I walk straight to the large desk in front of the window and test for locked drawers. There are none and that doesn't surprise me. Locked drawers are suspicious. If a wife finds a locked

Avenged Innocence

drawer, she wants to know why it's locked. Guys like Paul are more careful than that. I open each drawer and reach clear to the back, shuffling pens and papers out of the way. There is an official looking memo addressed to Paul with the Anderson Accounting Co logo that matches up with the internet info. It's not exactly a goldmine find but it is nice confirmation.

Then, in the bottom right-hand drawer, flush with the backing, my fingers close around an envelope.

Bingo.

I pull it out. Sure enough stacks of twenty dollar bills. Probably close to a thousand dollars' worth. Most people don't keep cash anymore. But addicts do.

I slip Pac off and carefully secure the envelope inside. This is what I'd been hoping for. Everything else I might find is gravy. The cash stash is the big reason that pill-popping is a box to check off before they become a mark.

It's also why I call it a transaction. I take their money as payment for ridding the world of their existence.

I won't take anything that their family would miss or that rightly belongs to anyone else.

That would be wrong.

The top of Paul's desk is bare except for a computer. I move the mouse and it reveals a screen with a password box. That's what I figured.

There's a desk calendar but nothing of importance written on it. And it's still laying open to May. It's probably just for decoration. Anything of importance gets put in a phone.

I hustle through the few papers that are laying in the drawer. There are credit card bills but nothing excessive. No charges to 'I'm a Molester Inc.' or something obvious like that. The truth is, guys like Paul are smart. The police have a hard time penning them down because they're careful. That's why it's hard to get the initial proof. Sure, once you have the evidence to dive into their computer hard drives and have permission to take apart their phone, you can unbury all their secrets.

But on the surface, they're extremely careful. That's why there are so many of them still out there.

But I don't need concrete proof. I only need to confirm my suspicions.

If they show up to a meeting expecting a young girl, they're sick.

All I know is all I need to know.

Paul pretended to be a kid. Tricked another kid into meeting him alone without mom or dad around and... well, there are no pure intentions.

And, in my opinion, no need for a trial. No judge. No jury. I'll simply serve as the executioner and save his wife and daughters the embarrassment of the courtroom drama.

Nothing else is in the desk. I should probably head back. I'll swing by the store and buy some food for Regina and the boys as promised. I exit out of the office and pass the stairs heading up to the second floor.

Upstairs is probably just the girls' bedrooms. Nothing I need to see... yet, I can't help myself. I'm pulled against my will. Some unexplainable force is propelling me up the stairs.

As I suspected, at the top of the stairs there are three bedrooms and a bathroom. The first door reveals a spacious guest room. It's decorated in the same sleek modern theme as the master. The girls' rooms are a stark contrast. But not in a bad way. One room, the nursery, is done completely in pink. I poke my head inside and the princess theme is overwhelming. The second room, the older girl's is decorated in lime green and purple. Very cute. The white furniture theme from the master carries through to both. There's even a little white desk with a 'family' calendar hanging above it. Next week is highlighted with 'Nana and Papa's with Mommy'. The library story times are all written down along with a few play dates.

So innocent. So precious.

I have wrestled with the balance of ending guys like Paul. I believe I am saving future victims from their cruelty... but

Avenged Innocence

sometimes they are actually good fathers. Monsters who care for their wives and truly love their own children.

But I reconcile following through with what I do by looking at it this way:

If Paul were arrested and exposed for what he really is then his daughters would be embarrassed and ostracized and his wife would be humiliated. This way (my way) the wife and children are spared the spectacle. Instead of being rejected, they are embraced by the community. They are loved and supported. My way ends up being better for everyone.

I look at Haylee's bed. Tucked in neatly with the bright green pillows on the purple comforter is a big brown teddy bear. About the same size as Jewely but this one isn't bedazzled. My mouth curls up ever so slightly thinking about my treasured bear. I had slept with her every night since Daddy gave her to me; I even took her with me to the hospital when….

CHAPTER 19

My reminiscing comes to a screeching halt when the front door opens and a little girl's cry shatters the silence.

Then I hear a woman's voice, soft and reassuring.

Damnit.

I take three large steps and ease into the guest room just as footsteps start up the stairs.

"But my dress…. My dreeeeesssssss."

"It's ok Haylee, we'll change into another dress and we can still meet Molly and her mom for lunch."

"BUT I WANT THIS DRESSS… and now it's ruined!"

"It's not ruined sweetie. It was only water. This is why you can't take the lid off your cup. C'mon honey, hurry up. Katy is sleeping in the car."

My heart is pounding so loudly I'm sure they can hear it.

I try to take slow even breaths.

A ringtone echoes down the hall.

"Haylee, slip this on. Hold on one second, it's your daddy... Hey sweetheart... Oh we're doing okay. Haylee spilled her water on the way to the library so we ran home to change before we meet Steph and her girls for lunch. How's your day going?"

There is a pause then she continues in a noticeably down-tick of a tone, "Again? Okay. Yeah, it's fine. We'll just order pizza or something. Don't worry about it. We'll see you tomorrow."

Avenged Innocence

She seamlessly switches back to the mothering tone.

"Good job, Honey. Thank you for being patient. Daddy has to stay in the city again tonight."

"Another meeting?"

"Yep, another meeting. C'mon let's go."

"Mommy I'm hungry…"

I hear the voice fade out as they trot down the stairs.

I let out a giant exhale.

I've never had a close call like that before. I strain my ears to listen for the car doors shutting and for the van to leave again but I can't hear anything. I creep over to the window. The driveway is empty. I'm assuming the coast is clear.

I wad the garbage bag into a ball and shove it in my back pants pocket. No more snooping. I got the cash, now I gotta go.

I bound down the steps with Pac bouncing heavily on my back and I sprint out the back door.

I run past the tree house to the front of the for-sale house and onto the sidewalk.

I continue walking quickly until I'm on the highway. Then, once I'm surrounded by the comforting traffic, I finally slow down my steps and my thinking.

I have a weird feeling about the phone call. A nagging in my gut. But that could be the nervousness from Gretchen coming home.

There is no way I can make it downtown to follow Paul wherever he's gonna go.

Maybe he does have a meeting.

Ugh. But I don't think so.

Maybe he's just cheating on Gretchen… I can only hope.

I need to get cleaned up again. The combination of the recent stress and the rising temperatures make me keenly aware that I'm sweating profusely.

I swing by the small gas station and gather up my clothes that are now dry.

Now to figure out where to freshen up.

I'm too far from my favorite truck stop but I did spot a hospital on the way back to the commercial area.

Hospital bathrooms don't tend to draw much attention because everyone is distracted with their own reason for being there. Most people mind their own business so it's easy to get in and out. Plus, the bathrooms are almost always clean.

But I hate hospitals.

Unfortunately, I don't have much a choice.

The sun is already hot on my face and shoulders. I can feel my shirt clinging to my back underneath the weight of Pac.

The rest of today I'll shower and get cleaned up. I'll buy food for Regina and the boys.

Tomorrow I'll stake out Paul's office.

CHAPTER 20

I see the hospital sign. Right before the massive building, sits a small strip mall. The occupants are a pizza chain, a tax office, and a salon that is adverting $7.99 haircuts. Beauty maintenance isn't usually an indulgence I can afford but I think I've earned it.

I deserve to splurge a little.

First I'll get washed up, and then I'll get a haircut.

I cross the busy intersection to the hospital, trying not to look out of place. I walk in the emergency room doors and pretend to know where I'm going. Purposeful doesn't get questions.

The smell of disinfectant and sickness assaults me as soon as I enter the waiting room.

I hate hospitals. Every time I'm in one it reminds me of the last time I saw my dad... or what was left of him.

He had loved his job as a fireman. He loved helping people. That night when he had left for work had been like any other night. It was only a few weeks past my birthday party. He was on a stretch of overnights.

He gave us all hugs and kisses on his way out the door and made a request for bacon and eggs when he got home in the morning. Then he winked at me and said, "Actually, I'm feelin french toast... or maybe cinnamon rolls. I'm in the mood for somethin' sweet." Then he swatted my mom's backside before wrapping her in his arms and kissing her neck. They both laughed and mom watched him walk all the way to his car and drive away before going back to cleaning the kitchen.

A little while later, mom tucked me into bed in the wonderful way that mothers do; two books, two songs, and then she lay beside me and played with my hair until I feel asleep.

The next thing I remember is mom rushing me out of my warm bed that she had secured me into just a few hours before. She was carrying Riker. William was stumbling out of his room.

"We have to hurry. There was an accident. Daddy's hurt." Mom cried.

"A fire? Was he hurt in a fire?" At eleven-years-old, William was the only one of us kids to appreciate the gravity of what was happening.

To Riker and me, our daddy was a superhero. He couldn't get hurt.

But that ideology was shattered after we raced through the sterile corridor and down the empty hallway.

We smelled the rancid burning flesh before we even stepped into that hospital room.

My daddy, a strapping 6'4 bulk of a man, lay helplessly on the bed. So withered away he was unrecognizable. The bits of skin that remained were hanging from his body.

His limbs were fastened to the side rails.

His eyes were glazed over.

Two doctors and two nurses were at his bedside. Their faces were grim.

My mom dropped Riker as she fell to her knees beside Daddy.

Her wail pierced through the stifling silence.

I remember thinking it was a dream. A terrible, terrible dream. It wasn't really happening.

William had scooped up Riker and brought him by the hand over by me.

We stood there in the doorway and watched Mom's body heave with sobs as Daddy took his last breath.

Her screams echoed through the whole hospital.

Avenged Innocence

The moment was surreal.

I have no idea how long we stood there, my brothers and I, witnessing the fate of our family change drastically right before our eyes. None of us would ever be the same.

William's hand squeezed mine. I looked up at his face, somber and more grown up than I'd ever seen. Looking back, I think he knew in that moment that he would have to grow up quickly. In that room he transformed from a boy to a man. Much too soon.

I know he cried. I know he missed Daddy too but from that night on, my big brother was the man of the house.

He helped shoulder Mom's burdens. He tried to guide Riker and me through the difficult time. That's another reason I had to leave the way I did. As much as I knew it would pain my mom and brothers to lose me, I knew that not knowing would be worse.

This way, this way at least they had closure. They could mourn and move on. And I hoped and prayed they had. I have to believe they moved on. I hope they had accepted the terrible reality I had left for them and that they had banded together like we did after Daddy died.

I round a corner in the unfamiliar hospital and feel a spark of happiness. There is a family restroom sign.

The jackpot of commode privacy and it's exactly what I need.

The hospital bathroom is large but unremarkable. I quickly slip off my black shirt and use it as a washcloth for my face, arms, and belly. I slip on my extra shirt while my skin is still damp. Then I shimmy off the big jeans and panties. I quickly rinse off the rest of my body. It's not as satisfying as a shower but I do feel better.

I slip on a clean pair of panties, my jean shorts, and converse and; "Ta-da", I'm refreshed.

I splash water on my face again and brush my teeth.

A knock on the door.

"Be right out."

I'm almost done. I wring out the clothes, zip up Pac, and walk out as nonchalantly as I can. I didn't do anything wrong but I feel like I look suspicious.

I hurry out of the hospital and back across the street to the promise of a haircut for less than ten bucks.

The door to the small shop dings as I walk in.

I'm not gonna think about Paul, my family, or even Regina and the boys. I am going to shut down and simply enjoy the next thirty minutes of normalcy. I'm just a teenager getting a cheap haircut.

CHAPTER 21

I walk out of the chain salon feeling like a new person.

I had opted for a shampoo and a trim. I passed on the blow-dry and style. It seemed like a waste of time and money since I'm just gonna throw it back into a ponytail anyway.

I noticed a small grocery store on the way back to Regina and the boys so I swing in to buy the food I had promised. Pop-Tarts, granola bars, and beef jerky. That's almost all the food groups.

I would love to offer to treat everyone to a meal at BK but I'm afraid that would make Regina suspicious or maybe even offended. I walk briskly to the corner; the sun is starting to set. I didn't realize it was getting so late. I get to the underpass just as Regina is getting to the boys.

She greets me with, "Didn't know if you were gonna make it."

"Yes ma'am." I realize as I'm saying the words that they don't make sense but she ignores it and asks, "Been busy lookin for work?"

"I've been busy figuring out next steps." That's not a lie.

She gives me a skeptical look but makes a gesture for me to sit next to her on the ledge. She goes through the same routine as the evening before, sorting through the box as both boys look on or read.

I hand her the bag of groceries I purchased. She takes it and sorts out the contents with the rest of the goods. Had I been expecting a 'thank you', I would have been disappointed.

When she finishes we make our way to the church. The same drill as last night. Even though it's only happened once before, it already feels like a routine.

I watch Regina walk. Her body, not very old, carries itself with an invisible weight of stress.

The boys walk obediently behind her. I want to know their story. I want to know how long they've been out here, how they got here, why they're here, who they are.

But I can't ask.

Not yet.

"You'll help tomorrow?" It was a statement with just the slightest uptick to classify it as a question.

I had wanted to go to Paul's office tomorrow. I'm getting to the fun part: figuring out his routine and planning the transaction. But I have no idea how long that will take. Until it's complete, I need Regina.

"Sure. Just tell me what to do."

"You hold a sign. You take what they give you. It's not too complicated." She peers at me over her shoulder. I had meant it as quippy, not literal, but apparently we're not on the same page yet.

"I can do that."

Again, nightfall happens quickly and we slip into the church under the cover of darkness.

Down the stairs then into the small living space. Everyone goes to their assigned section, including me. The boys settle quickly.

It's a comfortable silence as we all open our books and get lost in other people's stories.

Just like last night, I drift off into a peaceful sleep.

Avenged Innocence

Once again, I wake up to the delightful scent of coffee.

I could get used to this.

The boys are stretched out, their lanky frames taking up a good portion of the floor space.

They're quietly chuckling about something in one of their books. Ribbing each other in the beginning stages of a rough and tumble match teenage boys get into. But it never escalates that far. They settle back down and continue reading.

I don't know how they secured this church as a temporary residence but it seems to work well.

I sit up and stretch. My body is cramped from curling into the corner and my neck is kinked from the weird angle, but I feel rested.

Regina pulls her lips back, close to a smile, and tilts her head forward in a curt courtesy nod.

When she speaks, her tone is matter-of-fact yet mothering.

"Take a minute to enjoy your coffee… then we move."

I do enjoy it.

Deeply breathing in the rich aroma before taking a drink and letting the full, hot, rich liquid run down my throat.

I hadn't had a taste for coffee before leaving home but I quickly developed a love for the warming beverage during my first winter on the street.

Coffee is social. When you're cold and alone, the hot beverage (and company it brings) is welcome.

I look at the boys who are both engrossed in their studies. I notice little remnants of donuts on the corner of the mouths. And also the absence of facial hair. I had assumed both to be in their late teens, but wouldn't they need to shave if that were the case?

My mind starts to formulate more little tidbits about the trio to piece together some of their story… but I have a niggling in the back of my conscious. A pestering need to check my phone. Usually I'm not tempted because the cons outweigh the curiosity. But I feel like I can trust Regina and the boys, plus my anxiety over Blue Bunny is starting to build. I feel like something is wrong. I have a pit in my stomach. I know he's bad news. I know it.

I wonder if he's messaged again. I really want to check....

But no. Better not. I should still ere on the side of caution.

I lean back against the wall. Pac under my knees as I watch and listen to pick up clues to this family dynamic.

But they offer none. Regina quietly reads the same book as yesterday and the boys seem to be engrossed in the 'Secret Lives of American Presidents'.

I finish my coffee and stand to stretch.

Regina looks up and seems to take this as a clue for her to get mobile as well. When she rises, both boys immediately roll over and begin putting away their sleeping quarters.

I slip Pac on my shoulders.

"Might be easier to leave that here." Regina says, nodding to Pac.

"Nah, I'm alright." I meet her gaze, the rest of my face unmoving, and she drops it.

She grabs a sign, a small cardboard box, and another coffee tin from the corner closest to her sleeping area. The sign is nothing fancy. It's one of the flaps from the box and it mimics Regina's. 'Hungry. Homeless. Anything Helps. God Bless."

She tucks my materials under her arm and, once again, we head silently up the stairs, out the door, and towards the interstate.

This time Regina falls back and lets the boys lead.

"You worked a sign before?" I assume that's her way of asking if I've begged on a corner.

"A few times." The full truth.

"Every little bit helps. You say thank you every time and you don't guilt no one. If they got extra and wanna give it, we appreciate it. If they don't got it or don't wanna give it, well that's fine too."

"Yes ma'am."

Avenged Innocence

She sets me up on a corner at the exit of the 7-Eleven, about half a mile before we get to the interstate.

"You can walk over this afternoon for a break."

That's her version of a departing line. Then she and the boys continue on their way.

One of the little tricks you learn when asking people for money is to be as convenient and accessible as possible.

Regina switches with the traffic. She waits at the stoplight leading to the onramp in the mornings. Then in the evenings she'll switch to the bottom of the exit ramp.

I was honest when I said I'd only done this a few times. It was in the beginning, when I didn't have any other options. It was a wake-up call for the types of people that are in this world.

I thought my starting-a-new-life plan had been flawless.

It was mediocre, not brilliant.

It had worked, but at fifteen, I hadn't taken into consideration how truly awful some people can be. I thought Clearing Boy was the scum of the earth. He was; but he was far from alone down there.

The first time I ran out of money was about a year after I left home. I had been frugal but I hadn't realized how expensive it was to be homeless. I thought the money I had brought with me would last a lot longer. I also thought I'd make a transaction sooner. I had shifted from boys to men and the complexity surprised me.

I had envisioned living a life of solitude, which I did (and continue to do) to a point. But I quickly found the need for community. Not even a month after arriving in Dallas I woke up with a knife on my throat. He took all my money from my wallet. Thankfully I had my Altoid stash hidden away.

That was when I made my first sign.

It took me a full eighteen months to replenish my funds.

In the meantime I had to resort to street signs and begging.

Everything was harder than I had anticipated

It didn't take me long to discover the full gambit of the human spectrum.

Hateful and judgmental looks from people glaring at me through their windshields.

Sympathy and graciousness of others as they offered food and cash out of their windows.

I hold up Regina's sign and mindlessly walk up and down the short rows of cars stopped at the light in front of the gas station. I don't make eye contact but if a hand comes out of the window, I take whatever it's bearing and respond with a sincere thank you.

I have no idea how much is in my coffee can but there are four or five blessing bags in the box along with the water bottles, pretzels, and granola bars.

Traffic has slowed considerably and I decide to swing into the 7-Eleven before heading over to Regina's set up. I set the coffee can in the box and carry both with me into the gas station.

I walk directly to the restroom sign in the back corner of the small store.

I duck into the tiny bathroom. Bathroom is an overstatement. It's more like a dark, dingy closet with a toilet. I set down the box in the corner and lean Pac against the wall on top of it (no way I want to set it on the floor) and I take out my phone.

I need to see if there are any more messages from Blue Bunny. Any clues to who it is or how they know me. But when I turn the power on, even though my phone is on silent, it dings.

The screen lights up and my heart drops before I even open the app.

I look at the notification on my home screen.

Bile rises in my throat.

I know. I just know....

CHAPTER 22

An Amber alert came across late last night.
A little girl.
Nine years old.
She went missing thirty miles from here.
Last seen at school yesterday.
She didn't get on the bus to go home.
I know it was Paul.
It never occurred to me that he may be scouting more than one target.
I can only manage one mark at a time… I guess I assumed that was the case for everyone.
I stare into the cherubim face of Angela Walker on my screen. She's a pretty girl with delicate features.
Tears sting my eyes.
I know this should strengthen my resolve. It should motivate me to act faster. But the opposite occurs.
I'm paralyzed. I stand staring at the picture of the little girl with the enchanting blue eyes and pink bowtie mouth.
Tears are streaming down my face.
That poor girl.
Her poor family.
I wonder how many daughters Paul has ripped away from their loved ones.

How many little girls he has sacrificed to fulfill his desires.

I can picture Angela's mother.

Her body shaking as she lays on her daughter's bed, probably holding Angela's favorite stuffed animal.

Sobbing into her little girl's pillow.

Angela's dad would be angry and broken.

Devastated that his little girl is gone.

Hating himself for not protecting her.

I wonder if she has siblings. I wonder if her parents will cling to them or if the pain will be too great. Will they only see Angela when they look at her brothers and sisters? Will that make her parents pull away from their remaining children?

Then I think about Angela.

How she must have felt.

The excitement of meeting a new friend.

The thrill of acting so grown up.

Maybe she felt bad lying to her parents but she probably thought, "What's the harm? My new friend just has a present for me."

She was probably excited about it all day.

The secret bubbling up inside her. Knowing it was wrong but liking that exhilaration of keeping a secret.

Then walking to the meeting spot after school. Anxiously checking for messages from her friend.

Being disappointed when she couldn't spot her right away.

Then relieved when the app dinged, getting the message that her friend missed the bus, or had to stay after school, or some other generic excuse. But don't worry, her dad will come pick up Angela and bring her to their house. Then he'd drive her home later to meet her parents, if she wanted. Her dad would be wearing a red baseball cap and a Mavericks t-shirt.

That's when Angela would spot him.

Then approach him.

He would be kind and accommodating and get her into his black Nissan Maxima.

Avenged Innocence

And that's when her nightmare would begin.
The feeling of dread as she realizes something isn't right.
Then the panic when she tries the door handle and it's locked.
Then the terror as he does whatever it is he does to her after the car is stopped.

I turn and throw up into the toilet.
Now the resolve takes over.
Now a sense of urgency boils into my belly.
He will not get the chance to put another little girl through the nightmare Angela Walker lived through or the terrible death (which I'm almost certain that) she has already died.
I splash water on my face to wash away the tear streaks. I brush my teeth, hide my phone, pick up Pac, and head to meet Regina.

Between the food supply yesterday and the money I've gotten so far today, I think we're square for a bit. I need to spend the next couple days focusing on Paul.

I see Regina from a ways away. Walking up and down the side of the road, holding her sign. She doesn't look out of place but she doesn't look like she belongs either.
The clothes, the attitude, the puffs of hair bobbing as she walks, they're the reasons she stands out and the reasons she blends in.
I wonder, yet again, what her story is.
I go up with the boys and I'm not the least bit surprised to find them both reading.
I assume my spot and help myself to a granola bar and a bottle of water while I wait for Regina.
When she ventures back over, glistening with sweat, I give her a minute before launching into the speech I'd been preparing.
"I really appreciate you taking me in and letting me stay with you." I begin.

Elle Iverson

She looks like a woman with the weight of the world on her shoulders.

She sits, elbows on her knees, her head bent forward.

Her eyes slowly travel from the spot she had been studying on the cement up to meet mine

"Here." And I hand her the coffee can half-filled with crumbled bills. Mostly ones but there are a few fives.

She eyes it, wordlessly.

She does that a lot.

"I'll head back over there in just a bit but I thought I'd let you know I have some things I need to do the next couple of days. So I can't work here anymore. I understand if that means I can't stay with you, even though I'd really like to. You all are very nice."

I can feel all three sets of eyes on me now. The boys' gaze shifts back and forth between the two of us. They seem as curious as I am to see what her response will be.

After what has to have been a full minute she simply says, "What things?"

I anticipated that.

"Research." Truth.

"For what?"

"A job." Half-truth.

"What job?"

"I can't say." Truth

"Will it get you back home?"

"No." Truth.

"Will it get you off the street?"

"Maybe." Half-truth. If I get caught I won't be homeless anymore... I'll be in jail.

"You do what's best for you. What I said before still applies. No drugs. No friends. No telling anyone. My job is to protect these boys. I'm happy to help you how we can but they always come first."

"Yes ma'am."

Avenged Innocence

Then she points a finger in the direction I came from, "Better get back to it. Every dollar counts."

I obediently grab the now-empty coffee tin and cardboard box and make my way to the 7-Eleven. But this time instead of mindless gathering, I'm formulating my strategy.

'One Week' by The Barenaked Ladies echoes in my head as I hold the sign and take the generous handouts.

I don't like putting time frames and deadlines on my transactions… but this one is different.

Because of Angela (and thanks to Blue Bunny) now I feel an urgency to finish up and get out of town. Out of state.

In a new town. In a new state. And I'll use a new app.

I'll start a new life with a new identity.

Excitement starts to creep in.

I can't help myself.

Even with the blind rage I feel for Paul, and the anxiety about Blue Bunny, there's still a small part of me that is exhilarated by the thought of starting over again.

It wasn't exactly easy to disappear the first time but I can do it again.

I have to.

CHAPTER 23

The next morning I am awakened by the smell of coffee. (The best part of wakin' up… and all that jazz.) I had been curious if this new treasured routine would end after the conversation yesterday afternoon but Regina's attitude hasn't changed at all.

She smiles at me as she sips her coffee. She seems to be in the same mood as the previous mornings.

When we leave to start our day, we walk in the same direction for a while. When we do part ways, Regina catches me off-guard by turning and embracing me.

"Be careful. Whatever you're doing. Be careful." She whispers fiercely into my ear. Then she pulls back, her face only inches from mine, checking for understanding.

Words escape me, so I just nod.

Regina and the boys head to the interstate and I prepare for the long trek downtown. I devised a plan, of sorts, when I was holding the sign yesterday afternoon.

It's not elaborate or complicated. It is simple. That's the key.

I'll watch Paul's office. Wait for him to leave. Then I'll watch his house. Figure out his routine.

I will do that for a week to get a feel for how his days go and find a window of opportunity; that's when I'll finish the job and bolt.

Avenged Innocence

Any illusions I had of escaping Blue Bunny by hauling tail and just forgetting about Paul vanished when he took that little girl. I have to, *have to*, make sure he never hurts anyone again.

The online info and the paper I found in his office both indicate that he works at an accounting firm in a small business district. It's a location I definitely don't belong but I'm hoping to find a coffee shop or someplace where I can camp out and watch.

My other dilemma... how to get there?

Paul's office is about five miles further past his house from the church.

That makes it an eight mile trip.

I could walk. I could. But it would probably take me all day

I hate the idea of buses. Too many people.

Uber is my best bet, though I hate spending the money.

But the reality is; I want to see him to go to lunch so I can make sure I'm in the right place, but I can't make it there in time on foot. Most of his lunch picture posts were made before noon. Which means he probably goes to lunch about 11:30.

I hate working on timeframes.

Uber it is.

I glance behind me. Regina and the boys are out of sight so I head into the closest business.

A McDonalds.

I open the doors and the smell of McGriddles clings to my skin. Grease. I smell grease and fried food. My stomach rumbles, begging for a breakfast sandwich and hash browns. But not today. If I'm coughing up money for car fare then I have to skip the treat of a hot meal.

Once I'm in the bathroom (my reprieve) I go to the handicap stall, set Pac on the changing table, and get out my phone.

I turn it on but can't bring myself to open the app.

Not yet.

Yes, the technology makes my job easier... but only because sickos like Paul have the same idea. I don't know for sure that this is the way Paul found Angela, but I do know it was him who

Elle Iverson

took her. It all adds up. The "working late" phone call to Gretchen, the frustration he felt from being stood up a couple days before, and the fact that she went missing right after school (his same play with me). Yeah. It was him. I'm sure of it.

What I can't be sure of is how he arranged the meeting.

I think PlayRound is a pretty good guess.

Which is why I stare at the icon on my phone and fight back the bile rising in my throat.

I need to find a balance between using Angela for motivation without letting the thought of her (and the other victims) paralyze me.

To stall a little longer, I click on the internet icon. I need Paul's work address to fill in the Uber destination.

The opening headline offsets my best efforts to not throw up. I turn around and heave into the toilet.

"Body found of missing girl… Police have identified the body Angela Walker, age nine, who was last seen…"

I flush the toilet and sit down on the disgusting floor. Putting my head in my hands.

Even though I had strongly suspected that he had killed her, I still felt my whole body go lax with grief at the confirmation that the little girl was gone.

I can't think about that right now.

I need to stay focused on my newly expedited mission.

I wipe my eyes (and my mouth) on my arms.

I zone out as I get my toothbrush and toothpaste out of Pac.

Then I brush my teeth.

I brush them until my gums bleed.

I spit, put everything neatly back inside Pac, then reengage.

I pick up my phone and continue with my original intent of opening up the search browser. I find Paul's work address and look for a destination close by. There's an outlet mall not far from his business development.

Perfect, I'm just a college kid out to do a little shopping.

Avenged Innocence

I open the Uber app and request a ride. I'm relieved when a young woman about my age pops up as the driver. According to her profile, her name is Lexi. She's pretty. She has a round face that is accentuated her short brown hair. She has large brown eyes that are magnified by the thick-framed glasses she's wearing.

The likelihood that Pendar (the silver van guy who had initially escorted me to Paul's house) would be dispatched here was almost nonexistent, but you never know. I'm just glad Lexi will be the one picking me up in five to ten minutes, driving a red jeep.

I use the little time I have to continue freshening up; washing my face and combing my hair.

I decide to change back into my college clothes and I'm pleased to find that the dumpster stink (from where they were laid out to 'line dry') didn't stick.

After a quick once-over in the mirror I head outside. Across the parking lot is a bench. It looks like an employee 'smoke break' area and it will work perfectly as my 'wait for a ride' area.

After I get situated, I make myself check PlayRound.

Only one letter. Nothing from Paul. Nothing from Chicken. Just Blue Bunny.

Before I get a chance to open it, a red jeep turns into the parking lot.

It comes to a stop right in front of me.

Lexi is driving and she offers me a wave and a smile.

I slide into the backseat on the passenger side. I know some people like to ride shotgun, but that lends a familiarity to the situation that I prefer to avoid.

The jeep smells of leather and cinnamon.

It's a newer model. Nice and clean. My legs stick to the seat as I turn to close the door.

Before I even buckle up, the peppy driver (who has been watching me with a cheerleader smile plastered on her face) says, "Hiya!" in a singsong tone.

She's friendly.

No, that's not the right word. She's more than friendly, she's energetic. She reminds me of a windup doll... who has been popping Prozac like Tic-Tac's.

"Hey." My enthusiasm doesn't even come close to matching hers but I'm hoping it comes across as cordial. I don't know if I have the energy for this.

"We're bookin it downtown?" The volume of her voice matches the eagerness and takes me aback.

"Umm, yeah. Please."

"You got it, Dollface!" And she shoots me a smile over her shoulder as she spins around and throws the car in drive. I watch her in the rearview mirror and deduce the source of the cinnamon smell. She is chomping on a red piece of gum like a cow chewing its cud. It's obnoxious. I have to look away.

The ride won't take long at all. I should wait to read Blue Bunny's message until I'm downtown. Alone.

I don't want to get distracted. I need to get set up in a good spot to watch Paul. I need to scout out the building, look for exits, make sure his car is there, and find a good place to see the entrance and his car... a lot to do. Blue Bunny will distract me. Whatever the message says, I should wait to read it.

Even while I'm listing these reasons in my head, my hand is holding my phone and my thumb is opening up the app.

I tap on the letter and it opens up. I read the three little words and they fill me with all the emotions.

Dread. Anger. Confusion. Sadness.

And resolve.

Again the message is short, sweet, and to the point.

'He killed Angela.'

CHAPTER 24

"You alright?" Lexi's voice sounds worried and I realize my mouth is gaping open.

"Yeah." I exit out of PlayRound and force a smile to my lips.

So Paul did take her. And he killed her. But how does Blue Bunny know that? And how does Blue Bunny know I'm watching Paul? The questions bombard me, racing through my mind.

"Boy trouble?" Lexi asks.

"Isn't it always?" And I let my face fall into a look of despair that I don't even have to mimic. It comes naturally.

"Well, you lucked out 'cause in my car, I offer free pick-me-up pep talks and platitudes for the duration of the ride." Smile. Smack. Smack. Smile. "So is this a 'He'll come around, absence makes the heart grow fonder' speech? Or a 'You're better off without him' rant?"

Now my smile is genuine.

"Definitely better off without him."

"Good. Those are my favorite kind. Let me guess... he's selfish. Inconsiderate. Never texts you back quickly and you think he's interested in someone else. Amiright?"

I actually laughed out loud for the first time in ages.

"You nailed it. How'd you know?"

"Cause in my experience, all men are the same. I thought I had found a keeper, ya know, a good one. He even asked me to marry him… But I found out real quick that I wasn't the first girl he'd proposed to. He actually had a wife. I know, I know, pretty cliché. But the kicker was… are ya ready? He had another fiancé hanging in the rafters too. The bastard was married AND he was engaged to two other women. So yeah, I'm a little bitter towards men in general. Anytime you need to complain about the horribleness that is the male gender, well you just give me a call." Smile. Smack. Smack. Smile. "And we're here."

She puts the car in park and I count out the money from my wallet.

She turns to face me, the huge smile still plastered on her face, "Next time I'll fill you in on the story of how I busted the jerk. It's one of those tragic, love-story, comedies." Wink.

I hand her the fare and thank her. For the ride, yes, but for sharing her story also. It was a welcome distraction.

I haul Pac out of the jeep, sling it over my shoulder, and wave farewell to my new favorite Uber driver. I head to the nearest store that looks like some place a teen girl would shop. That means passing the Baby Depot, not going into the store where the window mannequins are wearing pantsuits, and setting my sights on Old Navy.

When I get to the entrance, I glance back to see the red jeep turning onto the highway.

I open the door for a mother and daughter who both have their hands full of shopping bags and coffee cups. Pangs of jealousy fester in my mind as I watch them laugh and walk through the parking lot. There's a magnetic bond between the two. A familiarity that is obvious even in the short stroll to their vehicle. They are walking so closely that their elbows bump with every other step.

I let the door swing shut and dig my hands into my pockets as I walk towards Paul's office building. I think my mom and I would've been close like that. I would love to call her, ask her to brunch, and spend the afternoon trying on clothes and laughing about inside jokes. I think we would've been close. Even after what happened to Daddy.

But not after what happened in the clearing. That robbed me of so much more than just my virginity and my innocence. It took away the ability for me to ever completely be honest with anyone. If no one really knows you, can anyone truly love you?

I'm pretty much resolved to the fact that I'll never know the feeling of being in love.

I love. I care. But I simply can't accept that anyone will (or can) ever love me.

I'm broken.

There's a fuse shorted out in my brain that makes me different from everyone else. It causes sparks and misfires that I will never be able to talk about.

I will never be able to truly confide in anyone.

And that's my cross to bear. It's something I have to deal with all on my own.

Luckily, I find joy in my brokenness.

There is a part of me that feels fulfilled when I experience the release.

A sense of satisfaction coupled with an epic high.

The high of all highs when I eliminate a dark soul.

Relationships, love, deep friendships, and family are the price I pay to scratch that itch. To soar that high.

CHAPTER 25

I see the business complex. It's the definition of a concrete jungle. There are three large impersonal buildings that face a large manufactured green space in the middle.

Sitting grandly in the center of the imported grass and flowers is a marble fountain. Benches surround it and trees offer shade. There are a few picnic tables and a couple paved paths winding through. The trails seem to connect to a larger scheme but I can't tell where exactly they go.

The buildings all look the same except for the large signs out front declaring which businesses are located inside each.

I scan down the first plaque and don't see Andersen Accounting Co., but it is listed on the second building. The one closest to the parking garage.

Now this is where it gets interesting. Trying to watch Paul and his car.

It's a little after ten in the morning so I have time to scope out the office before I decide where to set up my stake out.

My college girl outfit may actually make me more obvious than my homeless ensemble would have been.

There are quite a few unkept and disheveled people milling around pushing shopping carts with broken wheels, carrying large plastic bags. They are a stark contrast to those going in and out of the buildings. Most of the 'working folk' are clean shaven and wearing suits or, at a minimum, khakis and a polo.

No college kids in sight.

Oh well.

I take out my phone and pretend to stare at it as I circle around the complex, observing everything. At least I can play up the college role. There is a side entrance and a back entrance but neither look like they're used much. The back entrance is guarded by a dumpster with a partial fence on three sides.

The side entrance leads out to a small sidewalk that joins the larger one out front feeding into the massive concrete circle surrounding the fountain.

There is a tree-lined path joining this business conglomerate to the next one. There has been a huge push to get people active and (in an effort to support it) a lot of businesses are offering walking trails and encouraging employees to 'get out' on their lunch breaks.

Right now the trails are empty. I head over to the parking garage.

I glance around and no one seems to be paying any attention to me.

That's good.

I walk purposefully into the large structure; no one knows I don't have a vehicle parked here (or a vehicle at all). The cement walls come up to my waist. They're thick. I get the feeling I'm in a concrete tomb.

There are three levels. I scope out the first. There are only a few empty spots.

There's an enclosed stairway to my right. I make one loop around the ground level and spot Paul's Maxima parked in a corner. I verify the license plate, it's definitely his.

I want to check out the other levels as well so I head to the stairwell. Before I enter it, I notice a small closet next to the door. I turn the handle, expecting it to be locked. I'm pleasantly

Elle Iverson

surprised when I am able to pull it open. It's just a storage room filled with a few sparse supplies, caution tape, and traffic cones.

Interesting.

I close the door and push open the heavy stairwell door and head up.

I walk to the second floor. Since the door is solid, I brace myself for a loud thud as it closes behind me, but nothing happens. The doors must have stoppers on them. I look around this level and it is pretty full too. There are just a handful of spots left.

Finally, I head up to the third level. The sun is blinding as I step outside. There are only a few cars up here. A Jag, a BMW, and a Hummer. I can tell by the giant spacing between these parked cars that the owners probably don't want to risk door dings by parking with the middle-class peasants and their Prius'. All three pricey vehicles are on opposite sides of the roof. I walk to the edge and look down. On one side I see the tree-lined trail heading to the other business park. It's pretty secluded, a lot of turns where I could catch Paul off-guard, but there are two immediate problems with that.

#1. Getting him there.

#2. The foot traffic could be unpredictable.

I walk to the other ledge overlooking the office buildings and fountain.

Right here would be an excellent place to set up a stake out, except I have no reason to be up here if anyone asks.

I peer over the ledge that faces the interstate.

I could try to watch Paul from his house. Try to nail down a good time to encroach on that routine.

Maybe he goes on an early morning walk around the neighborhood or maybe he sneaks a late night cigarette on his back porch. Anything that would get him alone, just for a few minutes.

But his house is nearly impossible for me to watch unnoticed. The playhouse was a great one-time cover but it's too risky for a

<u>Avenged Innocence</u>

permanent solution. There's no hiding spot. There's no other foot traffic. There's no place for me to blend in.

Here at the office, there are a few different places I could alternate between. I could get my notebook out and pretend to be hammering through homework. If I get caught then I can move.

I could also go to the benches surrounding the fountain. There are a few vagrants still lingering around. They're probably waiting for the office workers to go to lunch, hoping to scrounge up a few dollars.

As if on cue, the doors to all three buildings open and suits start trickling out. Eleven thirty on the dot. I watch for Paul but I can't tell him apart from the other clean cut, well dressed, cookie cutter men filing out of the buildings. Maybe this isn't such an ideal spot. I wait another thirty minutes. Very few people come to the parking garage. No one comes to this level. It seems only a few are driving to their lunch destination; everyone else disperses along the walking trails. The businesses would be so happy.

The trails are definitely off the table now.

I wonder how many small restaurants are tucked in around these buildings.

The busyness slows down quickly. Everyone has settled in to enjoy their afternoon meal.

I see a lone jogger making her way under the shade of the trees. Most females are cautious when they run. Alert. Prepared.

Men typically aren't. They don't usually need to be.

This played to my advantage with my fourth transaction. I had nicknamed him James (Just Another Male Evil Sicko) but his real name was Lawrence Culpepper. He was a weasel of a man. Short, skinny, and in his forties. His drug of choice was Oxy.

He had friended me on the app I used before PlayRound. It was a regular social media site that was popular with kids and adults.

The initial set up was standard. I stood him up the first meeting and then followed him to his apartment.

He had been one of the easiest to scope out because his apartment complex sat in-between a laundry mat and a dive diner. And because he was a creature of habit.

He ordered the same breakfast, at the same diner, every morning at seven sharp. Then he was off to work as a hospital janitor from eight to four. Then he went straight back to his apartment and creeped on-line from four to seven before he left for a run at seven on the dot. He always jogged the same route. Exactly three miles on a trail very similar to the one I'm overlooking now.

After a few days of watching his routine, I switched gears and started watching the trails.

From six to seven there were usually quite a few people but after that it wasn't very busy. Which is probably why he chose to wait that long. As a general rule, perverts prefer solitude.

The path was tree-lined and shaded. There were a lot of turns and one blind spot.

That's where I waited. I left Pac behind a nearby tree and I knelt down just around the sharp turn. I pretended like I was tying my shoe and at seven-fifteen, when he rounded the corner, he almost ran right into me. Before he could put together what was happening, I turned and gave a hard upper cut to his man-bits with the palm of my hand. As he fell forward in front of me, I used the same move on his nose.

Before James even hit the ground I lunged on his shoulders and braced my legs on top of his.

I pushed both thumbs on his windpipe and used my full body weight to press my hands on his throat.

By now it had become natural. My body reacted automatically.

Blood was streaming from his nose down both cheeks, like red rivers.

I watched his eyes, beady and gray, as they bulged out.

The flicker of light faded behind them.

Unlike Clearing Boy, James didn't put up much of a fight. Even so, next to that first time, he was my favorite. Maybe

Avenged Innocence

because the setting took me back to that clearing. Maybe because James had no family to mourn him. Maybe it was because of the vile filth he had messaged to 'Britney' (my social media alias he had wanted to 'meet') just minutes before he left on his run.

It felt good to rid the world of him.

Even thinking about it now, my head is soaring. After James stopped struggling, I pulled him off to the side of the trail behind some shrubs. He had been small but it still took tremendous effort to lug his scrawny lifeless body to where it wouldn't be discovered for a while.

I checked his pockets and, as I figured, he didn't have any cash on him. Just his phone. I seized it and the key that was tucked into his running shorts, grabbed Pac and made a mad dash for his apartment.

I tried to look at his phone but it was locked. I assumed it would be. I didn't take it to use, I took it so it would take the police longer to ID him.

Still flying high, I unlocked his door and walked directly into his dark, lonely studio apartment. Purposeful isn't suspicious.

The 'decorations' were minimal and the place was tidy. His wallet was the only item on the kitchen counter and it had $200 cash in it, which I slid into my pocket. I quickly checked all the usual hiding spots; freezer, toilet bowl lid, under the mattress. No money stashes.

Then it occurred to me, he was single and he lived alone. He wouldn't need to hide money. I went to his bedside table and opened the drawer. Sure enough, there was a stack of twenty dollar bills next to a near empty prescription bottle.

I pocketed that money as well but I left the drugs.

I wiped down the phone and laid it on the counter. Then I wiped down everything I had touched and used the key to lock up behind me. Then I placed it on top of the door frame. I hoped the police would assume he left it there while he was on his run. Just in case they had a gung-ho detective on the case. I didn't want anyone to think this was anything more than a random attack.

That whole transaction was satisfying. Everything had gone according to plan. I'm hoping for the same with Paul.

A little before one o'clock there is another rush of people on the trails. This time everyone is funneling back into the giant buildings.

I want to hang around to see what time Paul leaves.

I won't make it to his house tonight but maybe I can make it back before he gets here tomorrow. I'll get an earlier start so I can get a feel for his morning routine. Maybe I'll have better luck then.

I saunter back to the ledge overlooking the trails.

Deserted again.

My wheels are spinning as I try to put together the final steps for my transaction with Paul.

The adrenaline is already starting to beat through my veins and quicken my heartbeat.

It'll be soon.

CHAPTER 26

Now that the lunch rush is over, I make my way to the fountain to wait until Paul is off work. I skip down the stairs two at a time, not an easy feat with Pac slamming into my back. I push open the stairwell door and turn to exit.

Then, on second thought, I open up the storage closet and place half a dozen of the cones in the empty parking spaces. I think I have an idea.

I walk into green faux park area and find an empty bench angled so it's facing the fountain and Pauls' office building.

I sit with Pac between my feet and take in the scene around me.

The sun is shining. Once again I've sweat through my shirt.

It's calm. The suits are resuming their day indoors.

The homeless crowd has also dispersed. They are either enjoying a midmorning nap or scouting out a prime spot for evening commuters.

I start to think through my plan. The traffic cones, the timing the…

I'm startled when someone walks quickly from behind and sits next to me on the bench.

Sits too close.

I'm on one end, and instead of sitting on the other end, he sits in the middle.

Elle Iverson

He's looking at Pac on the ground in front of me.

His knees are shaking up and down. His hands are folded in front of him, also shivering.

"What's in the bag?" His voice is shaky and his eyes dart to me and his right hand flicks his right ear.

That's when I turn to look at him.

"Spaz?"

He nods, his head bobbing in unison with his legs, his fingers batting at his earlobe.

"What's in the bag?"

"How long have you been here?"

"Few days. What's in the bag?"

His voice is inquiring, almost childish.

He's a few crayons short of a box anyway, but now he is high as a kite, blitzed, gone, tweaking for sure.

"Spaz, why are you here?" I've migrated quite a ways from where I had been staying downtown with the security of his group. It's even more of a trek for Spaz.

"Lee brought me. What's in the bag?"

"Are you hungry?"

He nods.

I unzip one of the outer pockets and hand him a beef jerky and a breakfast bar.

"Why are you here?"

"I'm helping."

"Helping who?"

"Lee."

"How?"

"Here. I'm helping here."

"Doing what?"

"Helping. What's in the bag?"

"Spaz, why are you here?"

"I'm helping."

This is getting me nowhere but before I can shift the conversation, he stands as quickly as he had sat down and meanders to the trail. After a few yards he turns and asks again, "What's in the bag?"

He doesn't wait for an answer before flicking his ear, turning his back to me, and zigzagging along his way. The long, greasy ponytail swaying as he walks.

I watch him leave and wonder what he's up to. It's unusual for someone like Spaz to move to a new place. Especially leaving the comfort of his surroundings and the security Lee and his people provided.

Peculiar but not worth my time to ponder.

After sitting in the still environment for a while, reworking my plan, I opt against waiting for Paul to get off work. I don't think his evening routine will matter anyway.

Instead, I decide to get back to Regina and the boys.

Her warning plays in my head, *"We'll see you between six and seven. If you're late, don't bother coming back at all."* It's at least a two hour walk back. I can't afford to spend more money on an Uber. I don't want to spend the night here, at least not yet. I'm sure I could find a place to crash close by (eventually I will have to in order to finesse the plan) but not tonight.

At three o'clock, I head out.

The walk is uneventful. I play my game (and a Fall Out Boy medley in my mind) to pass the time.

Whenever Blue Bunny starts to creep into my thoughts, I shift my thoughts to devising the plan for Paul.

A little after six, I'm approaching Regina's 'office'.

It's funny to me how quickly things become normal.

As I near the underpass where the boys are waiting, a warm feeling spreads through my chest and a smile pulls at my lips.

I wouldn't call these three my family; but they are familiar. And for someone like me, who abandoned any semblance of routine or normal life, familiar feels nice.

The boys give me the standard greeting and I see the mirrored look of comradery in their eyes.

Elle Iverson

I take my spot and we let the silence hang comfortably as the boys continue to read and I watch Regina walk the line of parked cars until they slowly move through the green light and a new line pauses when it turns red. There's something about the way she carries herself. A humble confidence.

When the influx of new cars dwindles down to only one or two at a time, Regina gathers her things and joins us. She looks older today, worn out.

She offers a weak smile as she plops down in the space between Tyrone and me. Automatically she begins shifting through the box, sorting it out. I think she probably enjoys the semblance of routine too.

She passes out snacks, fills the backpack, secures the box back underneath the ledge, and we head down from the underpass in a single file line. I remember the way to the church now and I could find it on my own… but I won't.

It seems to be important to Regina that we walk together. I'm not sure if it's for control or piece of mind; either way, I'll oblige. We pass through the changes in the communities as the street lights come on one by one.

We get to the church just as darkness carpets the landscape.

Once we're inside, everyone settles in to read.

Routine.

"You changin' the world again tomorrow?" Regina's question startles me.

"Yes ma'am. That's the plan."

She tilts her head up a little, "You still keepin your research top secret? Workin on a cure for cancer?"

"Nope. Just tryin to figure out how to make a buck or two."

She seems to consider this and goes back to her book but I feel like now is my window.

"How long have you guys been on the street?" My question gets both boys' attention but Regina doesn't look up.

"Eight months, two weeks, and three days."

Avenged Innocence

The answer was matter of fact and doesn't leave room for more questions.

My curiosity is piqued, I wonder what happened. I don't peg her as a druggie type, but some addicts hide it well. I wonder if they are running away from an abusive husband or maybe hiding from a controlling boyfriend.

I have so many questions, but I guess they'll have to wait.

I pull my blanket under my chin and breathe in deeply. I know it's my imagination but I can still smell home in the worn fibers.

My mom's cooking, my brother's stinky selves after coming in from playing outside, my daddy's aftershave. I close my eyes and start fitting together the final pieces of my transaction with Paul.

The key points are starting to form but there are a lot of little details that need to be finessed. All the different scenarios to play through.

I have a few gaps to fill in. I'll need a few more days of checking out the office and his house but I think I have a pretty good plan underway.

I do enjoy this part.

The prepping, the planning, the plotting.

I picture the scene in my mind. I play through the whole transaction. Starting with the ideal Plan A. How it will go flawlessly from the initial attack to his final breath and my getaway.

My body relaxes.

My mind drifts towards sleep. But right before I slip into the peaceful side of unconsciousness, a thought crosses my mind that jolts me awake and will continue to keep me restless through the night.

CHAPTER 27

I must've dozed off and on because I'm roused from sleep with the same sentence that danced through my head all night.

How had it not occurred to me before?

Had I blocked out the underlying meaning?

Blue Bunny's message, 'He killed Angela.'

I had seen it as validation that Paul had been the one who abducted little Angela Walker.

But the realization of what that meant... That Blue Bunny was watching us, BOTH of us, that hadn't clicked until last night.

Who is he?

How did he find me?

And more importantly, what does he want?

This is the first time I'm the first one awake. I prop myself onto my elbows and look around, giving my eyes a chance to adjust to the darkness. The only light is a soft glow from a click bulb that Regina leaves on as a nightlight.

The boys are sprawled out, taking up half the floor. Their long lanky legs are intertwined.

Tyrone's book is lying by his head, still open.

I let my eyes scan the surroundings. Trailing over the shelves, looking at the food supply, glancing over the boys. When I get to Regina I jump. Her eyes are open and watching me. The whites

Avenged Innocence

are a stark contrast to the rest of her that is blending into the darkness. They are giving off as much light as the click bulb.

She sits up.

"C'mon. You can help."

She starts up the stairs. I tuck blanket into Pac, zip it up, and haul it over my shoulder as I follow her.

She holds the door for me and frowns when she notices Pac.

It's not that I don't trust the boys; it's that I don't leave Pac. Ever.

But I don't say anything, she has already turned away and I don't want to disturb the quiet of the morning.

I walk a few steps behind her. Regina has a leisurely strolling pace. She seems to be enjoying the dewy mist in the air. I also take a moment to drink in the perfect morning.

The simplicity of the sunrise is peaking over the horizon. The slight breeze is bringing the smell of a fresh new beginning. There is a calmness in it all.

When Regina does speak, her tone is kind but pointed.

"You don't have to tell me your story but I am going to tell you ours. For two reasons: Number one; so maybe you'll understand why I'm so set on our rules and so protective of my boys. Number two; so you don't ask any more questions around them. I don't need them wasting any energy frettin about the past. Their minds need to be focused on what's ahead and on gettin better, not worryin about the mistakes their daddies made."

I don't say a word but my mind reels at 'daddies'. Regina doesn't strike me as the promiscuous type.

We walk a bit further, she clears her throat.

"I met Michael's daddy when I was fifteen. You can just hold your judgement; it was love. Not puppy love. True love. We both came from good families. Hard workin families. And we was set to be the first from both to go to college.

Then, when I was eighteen, my mama and daddy were killed in a car wreck leaving me and my baby sister, Rochelle, orphans."

She's still walking a few paces ahead of me and I try to read the side of her face to find emotion but she remains neutral. Speaking of her parent's death with no more infliction than if she was giving directions to a local restaurant.

"It happened the summer before I was set to go off to school... but I had to take care of my sister. So I got a job instead. She was the only family I had left." Almost as an afterthought she adds, "My parents were both only children. My mama's folks were old when they had her; they died when I was a freshman in high school. My daddy's mom and dad weren't good people. We'll leave it at that. We were never allowed to see them. I think I met them once, maybe twice. Anyway, Rochelle was going into her junior year of high school and she didn't handle the accident well..." She let the sentence trail off, then continued regretfully, "Ya know, I think some people are built to handle crisis and some ain't. I'm not sayin' I was, but my little sister sure wasn't. She dropped out of school her senior year. Never graduated. I was working fulltime at the DMV and waitressing at night just to keep the house outta foreclosure and a little bit of food on the table. I couldn't..." For the first time I notice a quiver in her voice when she begins again, "I couldn't pay the bills and keep Rochelle out of trouble. She got mixed in with some gang and they messed her up bad."

Michael's daddy, Big Mike, he was going to a community college there in town and he was workin too. We got married when he graduated. I was nineteen he was twenty. He started his own company. We had Michael when I was twenty-three."

She stops talking as we walk into the gas station. It's run-down. The pumps out front look like they may have been the original ones. Like ever. The very first model; caked in grease and grime.

There are bars on the windows and cigarette butts lining the sidewalk to the entry.

Regina goes straight for the donut case, places two Long Johns in a bag, and then turns to the coffee counter. She hands

Avenged Innocence

me a cup and keeps one for herself. She places hers under the spigot of the carafe and fills it to the brim with the dark liquid before clipping on the lid.

I follow suit but leave room for a bit of cream and sugar. We walk to the counter and the older gentleman behind the cash register smiles and winks at Regina. "Fancy meeting you here."

"Mornin' Tom. Any news today?" He smiles even broader when she speaks to him, revealing a full set of yellowing teeth.

"Just that the sun started shining a little bit brighter when you walked in." Another wink.

My skin crawls.

I don't think he's a bad guy.

Just a creepy one.

I set Pac down and unzip my wallet from the front pocket.

"Please, let me get this."

Regina concedes and steps to the side so I can pay.

After Tom hands me my change, they exchange flirty goodbyes and we head outside. Luckily I have Regina with me so it'll be nice and bright.

We cross the parking lot and Regina picks up right where she left off. No small talk. No recapping.

"By the time Michael was born, Big Mike was makin enough for me to stay home with the baby."

She pauses, lets out a deep sigh, her shoulders shrug, and she sits down on the curb; like the next part of her story is going to take all the energy she has.

I sit next to her. The coolness from the night is still trapped in the concrete; it emanates through my jeans and cools my backside.

We gaze together across the rundown neighborhood. Our little church, encircled in its own little forest, is less than a mile away and I can see the steeple peaking over the treetops.

The wind has picked up a bit, swaying the branches, and whipping my hair in my face.

The hot sun beats down and beads of perspiration form on my forehead.

I take a drink of the hot coffee anyway.

It tastes delicious. I was a little worried that seeing the slum it originated in might influence my taste buds. Nope.

I glance over at Regina. Her knees are drawn to her chest and the palms of her hands are flush against her forehead. When she speaks, her voice sounds far off.

"Ya know, you never think it'll happen to you. Then when it does, it just does. And you don't even question it. You just deal with it and move on. Then another thing happens, something else that only happens to other people. And you deal with that. You do what you gotta do…"

Then one day, you realize you and your family been homeless for damn near a year. And Christina, I don't know how we got here." She slides her hands down her face and wipes her cheeks.

"We had Michael when I was twenty-three." Her voice was completely back to normal but her eyes were fixed straight ahead. Her tone was as if she were reading a script. "I hadn't seen my sister in almost three years. Then, when Michael was six months old, she shows up on my doorstep. Strung out bad. Lit up like a string of Christmas lights. Nothin but skin and bones, her eyes bulgin out of her head, her hair knotty and nasty, shakin and holdin a blanket. After the initial shock wore off, I tried to hug her. But she backed away, tripping backwards off my porch. She was skittish, like a beat dog. She was cowering and ready to run.

Then she threw her arms out and tossed the blanket to me. She didn't hand it, she threw it, wasn't careful at'tal. She tossed it. When it hit my chest, there was a small bump, it was kinda heavy. Not much weight but I brought my arms up real fast to catch it. When I looked up, my sister was gone."

I am watching her intently and it startles me when she turns her whole body towards me and locks eyes.

Avenged Innocence

"Christina, what I saw in that blanket will haunt my dreams until the day I die. Barely four pounds, like a shriveled skeleton, eyes shut, mouth open, the little chest heaving up and down trying to breathe; completely naked...it was a baby.

A premature, drug-addicted, malnourished baby boy.

I screamed for Mike, and he came runnin.

By now I was shakin and I knew we had to get to a hospital. Mike grabbed our car keys and baby Michael, and we rushed to the emergency room.

The baby didn't cry. Didn't make a peep. He just lay there gaspin, like a fish outta water.

Never opened its eyes. We was only ten minutes from the hospital but it felt like an eternity. And about halfway there, he quit movin. His little mouth hung open, his chest was still. I wrapped him up the best I could and held him tight. My tears soaked the blanket.

When we got to the hospital I raced through the automatic doors, sobbing and screaming "Help! Help!" Like a fool. Well a very nice nurse took the baby and ran away. Down the hall. I saw a swarm of people gather round.

One of the not as nice ladies come out from behind the information desk with a bunch of forms for me to fill out, and I did. I used all our information. I didn't have enough sense to lie.

Where it said patient name, I put Tyrone and used our last name. Tyrone is what I had wanted to name Michael, but Big Mike had insisted on a junior.

Mike come in with Michael and we waited.

The same nurse come out a little time later and asked a bunch of questions I didn't know the answers to. Then we waited some more. Police officers showed up. They asked a lot of the same questions. I gave them the same answers. It wasn't til the next morning that a doctor came and talked to us. It was a miracle the baby had survived. He guessed it was about a month premature, hard to tell exactly what drugs were in its system, but he thought probably heroine. His chances didn't look good, but they were doin' everything they could.

Then they took us to see him. He looked even smaller in the spaceship-type bed they had him in. I cried again, which made Michael cry. By now Big Mike needed to get to work. He was already a couple hours late.

Michael and I stayed at the hospital.

There were a few scares that first day. A few times it looked like he was fading... but that little baby was a fighter.

I didn't leave the hospital for a week. Big Mike brought me clothes and food. Social services come. Police searched for my sister. When they couldn't find her, they labeled the baby as abandoned. The doctor told us the bills would be massive. The care the baby needed, then and in the future, would be expensive. They asked if we wanted him put up for adoption. I couldn't. I hadn't even looked in his eyes yet but I knew he needed me. He was mine now. We started the long process of adoption before he was even released from the NICU.

Big Mike was hesitant at first; about a lot of things... adding another baby would change the dynamic of our family but he was mostly worried about the cost. The expense of the medical bills and the cost of raising two kids. But he came around..."

She laughs and it startles me. It was a cackle that grew into a full belly laugh and again, tears were running down her cheeks. This time she brushes them away with her fingers, still chuckling she composes herself enough to say "Big Mike joked about how he was worried that takin in Tyrone was gonna make us homeless." The belly laugh returns and she put her hands on her sides as if she was in pain. "That bastard joked about us being homeless."

In between breaths she manages to say, "I haven't told that story since we've been on the street. The irony. I never realized the irony until now."

She hoists herself up, grabs her coffee, and walks towards the church.

Avenged Innocence

That's obviously not the end of the story but apparently it's as much as I'm going to hear today.

It fascinates me. But it leaves me with more questions than answers.

Once again, I'm intrigued.

CHAPTER 28

By the time we reach the church, the boys are up. But they're not reading; they're playing bloody knuckles.

It's later than we usually leave so we hustle to put everything back in order.

We exit outside and walk together for a bit.

There is no hug when we part ways this time. Regina is focused on getting to work.

The boys nod as I wave and head out for my jaunt.

I had planned on venturing to Paul's office early this morning but it's already past eight o'clock now. There's no way I can make it before he does.

I decide to pull an audible. Switch it up. Instead of going downtown, I'll make my way to the library. I need to research a few things. I think I have a pretty decent plan concocted but there are a few facts that I need to check out. If everything turns out the way I think it should, then I have few supplies to pick up. Today is Thursday. Tonight I'll do a test run.

Monday is transaction day.

After that? Who knows?

I've worn out my welcome in Dallas.

I'll probably escape to one of the coasts.

I don't know who Blue Bunny is but he knows Christina and Christina can disappear a lot easier than Aurora did.

Avenged Innocence

Aurora.

I had never cared for my given name. My daddy had insisted on it. After having two sons, he was excited to have a daughter. A princess. As much as I hadn't liked my name growing up, it had been hard to change it.

But I had to. It was a no-brainer.

I need to blend in and a name like Aurora stands out. I had been tempted to go with another Princessy name; Belle, Rapunzel, Ariel, but none of them are exactly run of the mill.

I had let Ruger choose. He picked Christina.

Ruger is the only link between my two lives. Obviously I would have preferred no ties but it had been unavoidable. I wasn't worried about Ruger ever saying anything. His reputation depended on complete silence.

Knowing what I know now and seeing what I've seen, it's astonishing that my plan worked. From a sheltered fifteen-year-old mind, it was genius, but now I see all that could have gone wrong.

The plan I had devised on the way home from the dance after I had ran out on Levi is pretty much what I executed.

I had known I needed to feel that rush of the rainbow again. The intensity of all the colors. But I couldn't imagine harming anyone I knew. I didn't want to hurt good people.

Part of the thrill with Clearing Boy was seeing the evil flames in his eyes extinguish.

The irony in that analogy (the fact that he was one of the kids who started the fire that killed my dad) is not lost on me.

I also knew that what I was doing was wrong, but the thought of doing it again consumed me.

I knew if I got caught, I would be in trouble. But what scared me more, what made me decide to leave, was the thought of what would happen to my mom and brothers if I were arrested. We had been through such a hard time after Daddy died and we were finally getting back to living normal lives. If news got out that the teenage daughter of the fallen hero had a thirst for blood, it would destroy them and our family name.

So I went the route I saw as less painful and less ostracizing. I used the same reasoning with my disappearance that I use for taking away the pedophiles from their families.

Death is better than exposure.

Losing me would be less embarrassing, less damaging, than learning what I really am.

Again, the plan was simple. I would stage my own disappearance. But, at fifteen, I knew the likelihood would be high of them thinking I was a runaway, so I would need something more elaborate than simply sneaking away.

And my plan just so happened to allow me to feel the high and scratch the itch.

My plan wasn't foolproof. I didn't take into consideration all the things that could have gone wrong, but anyway, here it was:

The police had ruled Clearing Boy's death as a murder.

If a second murdered kid was found, I figured authorities would be on high alert.

Then if another kid disappeared, they would assume it was the same culprit, even if the body wasn't recovered.

I just had to find that second victim.

What better place to start looking than with the troubled kids my mom worked with? My mom was a social worker. After Daddy died, she worked from home a lot. I would overhear her on the phone with her colleagues and I would listen when she dictated her notes into a tape recorder.

I snuck into mom's office and thumbed through her files. I eavesdropped on her phone calls and dictations whenever I could. I was looking for red flags her cases; tortured family pets, injured siblings, only things that were serious offenses.

I started a list of names and addresses and kept checking in on her notes.

I was even able to follow a few.

Avenged Innocence

It took a lot of patience, luckily for me; I have always been a patient person.

I started squirreling money away almost immediately. Ten dollars here. Twenty dollars there. All of my allowance.

With every dollar, my heart got a little heavier.

I doubted myself a lot.

Many times I flat talked myself out of the whole thing.

I couldn't leave my family. I couldn't just cut ties.

I would get caught. There was no way I could live in such isolation.

I would try with my whole being to push all thoughts and memories of it out of my mind.

But that never lasted long. Soon, I would dream about Clearing Boy, dream about that first time. The memory would roll through my thoughts. As much as I hated it, I loved it too.

I would let my mind circle around it. I would let my heart race thinking about the last flicker of light in his eyes.

It became a compulsion.

I spent a lot of time at the library (reading but not checking out) books about serial killers.

Three or more kills, over a period of time longer than a month, constitutes a serial killer.

I had the bookends taking care of; it was that middle man that would be time consuming.

It was a whole two months after the dance before I found one I thought would check all the boxes. He was a seventeen-year-old boy who had been in three homes in as many months. He had just been removed from the last one because he almost drowned another one of the foster kids who was also living there. I heard my mom on the phone with the new placement family. She disclosed 'the incident' and also asked if they had any pets; apparently the home before this one had a cat that went missing while the boy was there.

His name was Conrad Harris and he sounded exactly like what I was looking for.

After mom went to bed, I snuck in and looked at the file.

There was no picture (which would have been nice) but there was an address. I knew enough not to type anything into my computer or my cell phone. When the final piece of my plan was put in place they would scour all my electronics looking for clues.

According to his file, he was only a few weeks away from his eighteenth birthday. He had been in and out of juvenile homes since he was nine years old.

My mom's job was draining but she usually enjoyed it. Yes, some stories broke her heart, but ones like this (where she was just shuffling someone around until they got kicked out of the system) drained her.

One night, I overheard her talking with her friend while finishing off a bottle of wine. They were talking about lost causes. She hadn't met many. My mom has a huge heart and looks for the best in everyone. (It's one of the reasons she's so great at her job.) But there are a few who are just bad seeds.

A few who are too far gone for any amount of love to restore.

A few who are broken at their core.

They went from the foster system to the prison system.

Not this time.

CHAPTER 29

By the time I was fourteen I had earned a lot of freedom.

I would tell mom I was going to Grace's house, knowing that she wouldn't follow up. But if she did and she discovered I wasn't there, I would say I misspoke and I had gone to Tara's.

Tara and I had a standing agreement that if either of our parents ever asked if we were with the other, the answer was unequivocally yes.

We were both sneaking out to meet boys… but for different reasons.

The troubled foster kid, Conrad, lived on the other side of town. I could have ridden my bike to check him out, but with the busy traffic I decided to try my hand at the bus.

Even on the way there, I was still trying to figure out exactly how I was going to pull this off.

The first time, with Clearing Boy, everything had just fallen into place. This time I would need to create an opportunity.

Should I use myself as bait?

I knew, if he was going to be the one that I would have to act quickly. He was only a few weeks away from turning eighteen and getting out of the system. After that, he would be much harder to track.

I found his address easily enough but no one was outside and it didn't look like anyone was home.

I walked by a few times, circled around the block and came to a playground. It was large and there were a lot of little kids on the equipment. There were also a few groups of older kids hovering around.

I had no idea what Conrad looked like but I jumped on one of the swings so I could observe. I put in my headphones but with no music playing so I could hear what was happening.

After five minutes of nothing, I was seriously considering forgetting the whole thing. Scrapping my plans, saying that I had an addiction to something like drugs, or maybe an eating disorder (something more socially acceptable) and asking to get help.

Addiction is addiction.

But I didn't want to get help.

I wanted to get high.

There was a group of boys to my left. They were joking around when one of them said 'Connie' and they all started laughing. Without hesitation, a dark-haired boy punched that kid in the stomach and stomped on his foot. The boy who had taunted him doubled over on the ground, curled his legs up, and wrapped his arms around himself.

Hmmm.

Just then, I knew how I could find out if that was Conrad.

I pumped my legs harder and harder, when it felt like my feet were parallel with the top of the swing set, I leapt off. I flew through the air and landed hard.

I heard a pop in my knee and felt pain sear through my leg. The group of boys ran over. Concern was etched on all their faces except one.

The dark-haired boy who had gut punched the other kid; he looked intrigued by my pain, not worried.

That's when I saw it.

The look. The same one from the Clearing Boy. My stomach knotted. My fists clenched.

Avenged Innocence

The other boys knelt around me but he remained standing. Like he was watching a scene but not participating. Purely being a spectator. I sensed the evil in him.

I left that day knowing that he was going to be my first planned transaction.

It was just a matter of timing.

Getting him alone.

I went back five times that month. Sometimes riding my bike, sometimes taking the bus.

Every time he had been with the other boys at the park. There were four of them in their group but Conrad and a boy with a gold hoop earring were always together.

I could tell by their posture and demeanor that they weren't the cool kids. They were hunched over, laughed too loudly, and talked too quietly. Most of the time they hung out by the swings until they would venture into the woods where they would smoke and drink.

One day, I couldn't find them at the park.

I walked around through the woods to the area where they would gather for their drinking and smoking.

Conrad and Earring Boy were the only two there and they both had their backs to me. I could hear a muffled crying. For a minute, I thought it was a baby or that they were playing a video game or watching a movie on their phones. Then Conrad shifted on his crouched legs, giving me a view of what they were watching so intently.

Laying on the ground in front of them was a small puppy. It looked like a mix of a yellow lab and a poodle. Maybe four or five months old. Conrad had one hand holding the muzzle closed, his knee was securing the body.

He took a long drag from a cigarette that was dangling from his lips and then he lowered it slowly, and put it out on the squirming puppy's paw pads. The puppy's muffled howl echoed in the quiet.

Conrad was harshly whispering at Earring Boy.

Earring Boy cowered in response. I got the impression that this wasn't his idea and he was regretting his decision to even be present.

Conrad slapped his arm with his free hand and Earring Boy picked up one of the puppy's back legs.

Conrad watched intently and said something else. I couldn't make out what it was, but Earring Boy dropped the leg. The puppy whimpered and squirmed.

Conrad shoved the puppy's secured muzzle toward Earring Boy who reluctantly replaced Conrad's hand with his own.

Then I watched in terror as Conrad, with one fluid motion, let go of the puppy's head and grabbed the other back leg with both hands. Then he pulled as hard as he could and, even from where I was sitting, I heard the hipbone pop out of place. The puppy screamed into Earring Boy's hand as Conrad moved immediately and repeated the torture to the front leg.

This time the puppy went silent.

It was probably in shock.

So was I.

I stared, frozen in place, as Conrad flipped the puppy over. Now using his knee only for leverage since there was no more struggle, he displaced both legs on the other side. The sickening popping sound ricocheted off the trees around me.

Earring Boy threw up. Conrad's eyes never left the limp body in front of him.

My mind wasn't registering what I was seeing. My body was rigid. My eyes were unblinking but unable to look away.

I watched in horror as Conrad lifted the puppy's head into his palm. He wrapped his finger behind its ears, like he was going to offer it an affectionate scratch but instead; he clamped his other hand on top of the puppy's muzzle and twisted with all his might.

Another skin-crawling, vomit-inducing pop and he let the head fall to the ground.

Earring Boy had already started back on the path. His legs shaky, he bounced tree to tree to keep his balance.

Avenged Innocence

Conrad stood, his eyes fixed on the lifeless golden heap in front of him. Then he kicked it. Maybe to make sure it was dead... but when the body remained unflinching, he kicked it again just for fun. Then he turned and jogged up the path toward Earring Boy, giving him a pat on the back when he caught up with him.

They walked together towards the park. My mouth had been hanging open and was now completely dry. I forced it closed and let my eyes trail back to the clearing. Hoping and praying that I wouldn't see anything. That the horror I had just witnessed was all in my imagination. But when my eyes fell on the still image of the small tan body lying lifelessly in the middle, I couldn't help but run to it. Tears streamed down my face as I fell on my knees and gathered it into my arms.

Now I could tell it was a golden doodle. The soft fur smelling of a recent bath. The scent of dog shampoo filled my nostrils as sobs choked in my throat. I clutched the puppy, like I would Jewely, nuzzling my face into its neck, its tongue hanging, dripping saliva on my arm. The legs dangled as the joints knocked against the displaced bones.

I don't know how long I sat there and rocked the poor puppy. It felt like hours, but in reality, it was probably no more than five minutes. Any doubts I had about Conrad vanished as I clutched the mangled body. I haven't been able to look at a puppy the same way since. Every time I see a lively, wiggling ball of energy, I picture Conrad holding it down and torturing it before discarding the poor thing like a dirty, old, rag.

I rocked that puppy and cried until the fur was soaked.

Then I cradled the limp body in one arm as I dug a grave for it with the other. I knew Conrad would do this again. And soon small animals wouldn't be enough. He would continue to torture, to escalate. I had to stop him. I had to do it soon. When the hole was deep enough, I laid the puppy down inside of it.

I dried my eyes with my sleeve then picked a few wildflowers and placed them on top of the small mound.

The rage bubbled inside me. Conrad was evil. There was no doubt about it. And the intensity in my heart with which I wanted to end his evil was one of the purest feelings I had ever felt.

It brought back parts of the rainbow before the transaction even happened.

Teasers for what was coming.

My body anticipating what it would be like.

I craved to feel all the colors.

Like drug addicts, with the shaking and withdrawals, that's what the next week was like for me.

Killing him consumed every one of my thoughts.

CHAPTER 30

I walk up the grand sidewalk to the library. Reminiscing had made the trip go by quickly. I pull open the door and go to the same spot in the back.

My heart is racing from remembering Conrad.

With the stress of Blue Bunny and the planning for Paul it had been a while since I have let myself relive one of my previous transactions.

I plop down in the chair and turn on my phone.

While that's booting up, my mind wanders back to Conrad.

I got my opportunity with him the week after he murdered the puppy. I had ridden my bike this time because I didn't want to make a habit of being seen on the bus.

I had found the group of boys, once again, at the park. I paused on my way to the swing set because something caught my attention. I walked over to it. A blue flier was tacked to a light pole.

A missing puppy.

Underneath the name 'Lucky' was a picture of a sparkling-eyed boy with a big toothless grin getting licked on the face by a tan puppy. It looked like a golden doodle.

A $500 reward was being offered for the boy's 'best friend'.

Tears stung in my eyes.

Anger filled my chest.

Resolve set in my heart.

I continued to the swings.

There were only three boys in the circle. (Well, technically that makes it a triangle, but the point is; Earring Boy was nowhere to be seen.) I wondered if he was scared of Conrad. Maybe he had finally seen what I saw in him.

After a little bit, the boys turned and headed to the woods. But at the last minute, the other two seemed to change their minds. They walked back to the street and Conrad slumped down the path by himself.

I knew that was my chance.

The rest was eerily similar to my first time.

I followed a good distance behind him down the familiar path to the small clearing.

I waited until he was sitting on a stump.

His back was to me.

He had a cigarette in one hand and he was scrolling through his phone with the other.

I knew I couldn't outright overpower him. Even though he was gangly, he was still two years older than me.

Not exactly sure of a plan, but in preparation, I had been carrying my mom's stun gun with me on each trip. She bought it for when she went running. It was small, light-weight, and easy to use.

I slipped it out of my pocket and cupped it in my palm. I slid the switch to power it on and kept my finger on the stunning button.

I circled around Conrad because I needed to approach him from the front. The gun wouldn't keep him down for long; it would merely throw him off balance enough for me to get into position.

I came into his line of sight through the other side of the path, looking distracted, doing my best to avoid eye contact and letting the insecurities I was feeling, surface.

Avenged Innocence

Conrad glanced up at me, I saw the recognition register on his face but he couldn't seem to place me. He looked down the trail behind me, took another drag on his cigarette, and then turned his attention back to the phone.

I took a few brisk steps, putting myself right in front of him.

My thumb on the button that would release a lightning bolt from my palm.

I hadn't actually used the device before but I had been with mom when she bought it. The clerk had explained to her that most people use stun guns improperly. They will only hold down the button for a second or two on a large area like the stomach or chest.

In reality, you should make contact with an area that has a higher concentration of nerves (chin, neck, groin) and hold it directly against the body for at least five seconds. This will momentarily incapacitate an attacker and dissuade them from coming back.

The roles were a little reversed, but I knew I had one shot and a small window.

Since Conrad was sitting down I decided to go for his neck. He looked up at me with sharp irritation as I stepped between his legs. I had the gun pressed under his chin before he realized what was happening.

I pushed the button. The shock that ran through my arm nearly threw me off balance but I leaned into him instead of falling backwards. This caused us both to topple over the stump. He landed flat on his back. I landed on top of him. The gun fell from my hands as I released it and exchanged my grip on it for a grip on his neck.

I braced my legs out just as I had done the first time.

Conrad's arms were longer than Clearing Boy's but he had a harder time controlling them since he was recovering from the shock of the stun gun. I had a few seconds to get in position.

My hands were in the upside down goal post formation and pressing straight down. Not up into the neck. Not down on the collarbone. Straight on his windpipe. I'm a fast learner.

I felt the colors rising inside me.

The blue fear of possibly getting caught.

The red anger for the puppy.

The green adrenaline from the whole experience.

I let them course through my veins.

When Conrad did regain control, his hand connected with my cheek in a hard and audible slap.

I bore down harder and used my legs to push his down. Also taking that leverage and using it to crush his throat.

His eyes got wide.

The same darkness flashed across his face that I had seen my first time. His arms flew up again and this time a hand connected squarely with my mouth. I tasted blood and felt a droplet land on my chin but I didn't move. Within another minute Conrad went limp but I still felt his pulse beating below my fingers. I leaned in further and tuned my ears to listen to any sounds around me. This area is not very busy (which is why the boys like it) but I still need to be careful. I had already devised a cover story if anyone happened upon us. Well, not so much devised as I had just planned to use the scenario from the first instance. A poor girl, lured into the woods by an evil teen. I had even thought of using Earring Boy as a character witness if I needed to. But all that ended up being unnecessary precaution because, just like when I had been assaulted the year before, no one came.

I continued to straddle Conrad while pushing down on his neck for a few more minutes. Letting myself enjoy the high.

Feeling the rainbow rush over me.

All my senses were on high alert.

My heart was racing out of my chest.

I stayed in place until I was sure the monster underneath me was gone.

Avenged Innocence

While I was staring at his face I realized a drop of blood had fallen from my lip onto his cheek. I licked my thumb and wiped it away.

I retrieved the stun gun that had fallen in the struggle and I looked around for any other evidence that would show I had been there. I didn't see any. My mind was racing now. What about hair? Or saliva? I hadn't considered that. And the scene would be searched. Especially if they connect it with the incident from last year, which I hoped that they would.

Worry and anxiety quickly dulled the rainbow.

I took the long way out of the trail, through the woods, which added a few more cuts to my arms and legs. As I rode my bike home, I tried to think of a reasonable explanation for the fat lip and scrapes.

When I was unable to come up with anything better, about a block away from my house, I crashed on purpose. Hard. Nothing fancy. I just turned the handle all the way to the side when I was peddling at full speed. Even though I was bracing myself for the impact, it still hurt. The tears were real as I limped into the kitchen and let mom bandage me up.

Mom got a call that night that Conrad was missing. They assumed he had run away again.

Until his body was found the next day.

The story ran on the TV while we were eating dinner the next night and I almost threw up my spaghetti.

I've done more than my share of studying serial killers, trying to understand why I am the way I am. A lot of them thrive on press coverage. They get excited about the media attention. It's some sort of power trip.

That has never been the case for me.

The 'victims' in my scenarios are truly predators, just undiscovered. The media doesn't know that.

As I sat there with my mom and brothers, listening to the report, I didn't almost get sick because of what I had done. (I was reveling in that.) No, it was the picture they were painting of Conrad that I couldn't stomach.

A school photo (that was at least a couple years old) of a clean-cut Conrad was plastered all over the news. The image of a harmless but troubled teenage boy who was taken from the world too soon.

It made me nauseous.

But I've learned that this is a trade-off I have to make.

The predators go out looking like prey.

Which I guess, in a way, they kind of are.

After all, I'm putting the finishing touches on a new trap for one right now.

Shifting back to the task at hand, I busy myself with my to-do list and dive into the final research.

Tonight will be the test run with Paul.

I only have a few loose ends left to tie up.

Once I finish here at the library, I'll meet up with Regina and get the wheels in motion.

I'm in the homestretch.

CHAPTER 31

I convene with Regina and the boys but only to offer to buy dinner and to tell them I won't be staying with them tonight.

I want to show my appreciation for her help and these growing boys need some substance. I also need a good meal. Tonight will be a long one for me.

Regina looks skeptical but agrees to a hot meal. She hides everything away and we venture to a hole-in-the-wall diner. The chalk paint on the front window advertises bottomless fries.

We walk in and are greeted with the sounds of cackling grease and clanging dishes. The scents of hamburger and fried food mingle in the air.

There is a sign telling us to 'Seat Yourself' so we pick a booth in the back.

The boys each take a side. Regina slides in by Tyrone. I sit by Michael, sliding Pac in underneath my legs.

The little restaurant is crowded and incessant chatter surrounds us, along with clamoring silverware and shuffling plates.

A waitress comes over with four waters in large, red, plastic cups. She slings them across the table, drops a stack of menus in the middle, and says, "Be back in a scooch."

She was out of earshot before I could even say thank you.

Her nametag read 'Meg'.

The frizzy hair (that is only somewhat pulled back into a haphazard ponytail) the smudged makeup, and her frazzled disposition hint that it is toward the end of her shift.

I take a sip of water and study a menu.

It is one page, laminated, and every item listed has a correlating picture.

And it's sticky.

This is a pretty classy joint.

Our table is the only one without conversation. We had sat in silence many times by now, but this time is different. There is an air of expectancy. Like conversation is sitting there, just waiting to be started.

Tyrone is fidgeting with his fingernails.

Michael is staring blankly at the wall above Regina's head.

I have a lot of questions I want to ask Regina. She had opened so many doors yesterday but I know none of them would be acceptable to ask when the boys are around. So instead, I turn to Tyrone and ask, "How's your book?" (Even though I can't remember which one he is reading.)

"Finished it." He replies quietly. "I started *A Comprehensive Educational Overview of Design Insight.*"

He answers my blank stare with, "It's a revolutionary book outlining the principals of Architecture. I want to be an engineer. Understanding the different aspects of the field will be advantageous in such a career."

A swift kick under the table to my shins reminds me to pick up my jaw. I wipe off the expression of surprise and doubt and replace it with encouragement and curiosity.

"That's really interesting." Is what comes out of my mouth while my mind's script is running through all the obvious reasons I doubted that dream would ever be realized. I feel two sets of eyes studying me intently. I am looking at Tyrone and his face is still turned down. He's winding and unwinding a thread from his t-shirt.

Regina and Michael are watching me.

Avenged Innocence

Judging my reactions.

The waitress returns and interrupts the moment.

She has her pen poised over a pad of paper.

"You first, Sugar," is her way of asking if we're ready as she smacks her gum in my direction.

"Uh, a cheeseburger and fries please."

"Easy-peasy. And you?" She cuts her eyes to Regina.

"Three more of the same."

"Piece-a-cake. Be back in a jiff."

I sneak another glance at Tyrone. He shifts uncomfortably then mumbles under his breath, "Michael wants to be a lawyer." Trying to divert my attention.

It works.

I let my eyes meet Michael's. When they do, he shifts uncomfortably next to me. "Yeah, I've been reading a lot of law books. The judiciary system intrigues me. I want to be an attorney but my ultimate goal is Supreme Court judge. Then maybe President of the United States."

I turn to look at Regina. Her head is raised high. Pride and determination are radiating off of her. I don't know what she's done or how she's managed to do it, but she has two boys who are in the midst of raging teenage hormones (not to mention the less than desirable circumstances) and at prime peak for rebellion; but instead of acting out, they are focused and driven.

Mad props to her.

The waitress, Meg, comes back with our food. I don't know whether to be impressed or worried by the speed with which our order is produced. They either have a chef in the back (behind the grungy looking serving window) who is quick, attentive, and proficient. Or they have a stock pile of burgers and fries prepared. By the look of the fries, I'm guessing the latter. They are off-white, soggy strings piled on the plate. Glistening with grease but still managing to be stale.

And we can have as many as we'd like.

Bottomless fries.

Clever marketing.

We thank the waitress as she plops the plates on the table.

Conversation comes to a standstill. When no one wants to talk about their past, when futures are so uncertain, and present circumstances are so undesirable... well, approachable topics are few and far between.

We eat in silence. I am surprised when I am the first one done. The boys seem to be enjoying their meals and savoring each bite. I break the silence. "I, uh, am gonna be moving on soon. Probably next week."

This gets everyone's attention.

"Where to?" Regina asks.

"I'm not sure yet. I thought about Vegas." Half-truth. "I'm actually going out tonight to scope out possible next steps." Full-truth, but misleading.

Regina's eyebrows raise in suspicion but she doesn't say anything. The boys follow her lead. I can imagine she has a lot of questions but she offers me the same respect I've shown her.

"Well, thank you for dinner." Is all she says while taking the last bite of her burger.

Meg scurries back over, shoving some crumbled bills in the front of her apron.

"Did ya'll save room for dessert?" she asks as she places the ticket in the middle of the table. But by the way she's clearing our plates and not listening for a response, it comes across as departing statement rather than a question.

Regina answers for the table, "No ma'am, but these boys sure would appreciate another plate of those fries."

Meg turns her wrist, makes a production of looking at her watch, and then mumbles under her breath, "Be right out."

Service with a smile.

I reach down and unzip Pac, feeling around the top, I pull out my wallet.

I had moved a few twenties from my savings tin to the wallet for easy access. The bill is just over twenty dollars.

Avenged Innocence

I lay down forty and say, "Keep whatever is left over."

Both boys stare into the scraps of fries on their plates. Regina dismisses me with a nod. The afro puffs on top of her head bouncing with the effort.

I grab Pac out from under the table and hoist it onto my back as I head out the door.

Back to business.

CHAPTER 32

The walk to Paul's is uneventful. My mind races with what could go wrong. That's one of the reasons I have test runs like tonight.

With my information being so limited this time, there are a lot of variables.

What if he stays in the city?

What if they are going out of town this weekend so he doesn't go to the office tomorrow?

What if Gretchen borrows his car?

But as I round the corner I breathe a sigh of relief when I see both cars parked in the driveway.

There are still lights on in the house; it looks like the kitchen and master bedroom.

I hurry to the car. I don't want to linger. The last thing I need is to be noticed, or worse, recognized. I ease over to the driver's side tire of the Maxima. I slip Pac off my shoulders and retrieve the small cylindrical object I picked up on my way back to Regina and the boys.

A flathead screwdriver.

The internet tutorial claimed that by unscrewing the air valve, placing the screwdriver on the stem and holding it down, the tire would lose air.

The online video had been pretty clear.

Avenged Innocence

Unscrew the cover, press down, there would be a hissing sound, and in a matter of minutes, the tire should be low.

I had debated which tire to flatten but decided on the front driver's side. I figure it has the best chance of being seen and, in turn, getting addressed.

I press inside of the valve down like the mechanic on the video had demonstrated.

The air begins to rush out of the tire. I whip my head around to make sure no one is outside. The noise is louder than I anticipated.

I watch the tire slowly (so slowly) lose air.

I need it to be noticeable but not suspicious. I thought about picking up a tire pressure gauge but had decided against it. I saved the couple bucks and would eyeball it.

When the bottom of the tire resembles a line instead of a circle, I pull the tool away and replace the cap.

Step one done.

I slide the screwdriver into the side pocket of Pac and rush to the street.

Now is where it gets tricky.

I haven't been to the office in the morning yet to see what time Paul shows up so I'll do the tire experiment tonight and another run-through on Monday.

I need to finesse the timing. That will be the key.

I have to be at the parking garage by eight a.m.

The walk from Paul's to the office will take about two hours but I'll find out for sure tonight. If that's the case, then I need to get to his place by six in the morning which means I need to leave the church by five.

Tonight I'll go straight to the office and find a place to sleep to make sure I'm there in time.

I walk as quickly as I can.

Breathing in the warm August air, doing my best to remain calm, and trying to think through the next couple hours.

Elle Iverson

The anxiety building in my chest seems to quicken my pace.
The trip goes by fast.
I walk through the business area.
It's dark but the security lights illuminate the buildings and cast a soft glow across the lush lawn.
The fountain is also lit up, making the atmosphere serene.
I notice a few people milling around in the back corner. There are four of them forming a circle. One of them has a long, greasy ponytail and he flicks his right ear as I walk past.
Spaz. I'm surprised he's still here but I'm glad he doesn't see me.
I have my sleeping arrangements narrowed down to either the quiet dumpster around the back of the building or the trees along the trail.
Resting beside the fountain would be peaceful but there are 'No Loitering' signs posted around it and those are usually enforced.
When people 'give thanks' for food and shelter sometimes it is done flippantly. It shouldn't be. I have to carefully weigh the risks of where I decide to sleep. Taking into consideration cover, safety, the likelihood of getting arrested…
I make my way between the buildings and down the small path. The area isn't very big.
I wonder how early someone will bring out the trash.
I need to get some sleep. I decide on the dumpster. I set Pac in the corner of the fence and lean against it so I am facing the only opening. I'll just rest my eyes here. Not bothering to take out blanket or anything else in case I need to make a quick getaway if anyone does come out the door.
The chill of the pavement goes through my jeans and runs from my butt up to my head and all the way back to my toes.
I curl my knees to my chest, wrap my arms around my legs, and lay my head on top.
I'll just relax for a minute.

CHAPTER 33

Clearing Boy is on top of me.
His eyes peering into my soul.
I'm violently kicking and scratching.
I can't breathe.
His hands are around my throat.
I shake my head to wake up.
I know this is a dream.
I've had it before.
I hate this dream.
I try forcing my eyes open.
There is a weight sitting heavily on my chest.
A wave of panic washes over me as I realize I am awake.
There is someone on top of me.
The end of a ponytail tickles my nose as my eyes adjust.
It's Spaz.
I'm flat on my back, parallel with the dumpster.
He's on my chest.
He's repeating something.
Chanting it like a mantra over and over.
"Just give me the bag. Just give me the bag."
His eyes lock on mine and they are wild.
Bouncing all over.
He is high.

He is beyond high.

He is frantic.

My head clears.

I quickly evaluate his position.

His hands are around my neck; but not in a lethal way. He is twisting, like he's trying to take the lid off a jar. It hurts but I can breathe. He has one knee on my chest and the other is on the ground next to me. He's heavy but unstable.

His eyes are wide and unfocused. They continue to bounce around my face while he keeps repeating, "Just give me the bag. Just give me the bag."

I take a deep breath. Or try to. His hands are getting tighter around my neck. Pulling the skin as he turns and twists.

"Spaz." I manage in a whisper. I'm clawing at his hands, trying to loosen his grip.

"Spaz! … It's me… Christina…"

But he doesn't register any of my words. He only continues his chant.

I curl up my legs, and with all the force I can muster, I arch my back and heave him towards the dumpster, throwing him off balance. His head knocks against the side making a loud 'clunk'.

I don't care who hears. The more noise the better. I hope the smash will stun him long enough for me to get back in the open where there are other people.

I lean down to get Pac and Spaz grabs my leg.

"Just give me the bag." He's looking at me; but not at me. His eyes are darting all over.

I yank Pac into my arms and try to kick away from Spaz's grip but he pulls my knees, taking my legs out from under me, causing me to slide down the fence. The wood scrapes my back and the concrete crushes my tailbone as I land hard.

Spaz scampers on top of me like a wild animal.

I reach into the side pocket of Pac and my fingers close around the cool metal of the screwdriver I had slipped in there just hours before.

Avenged Innocence

I pull it out and feebly hit him on the side of the head but he clearly has the advantage.

He's bigger.

He's in the dominate position.

And he is out of his mind.

I turn my hand sideways, making a fist.

I bring my arm back as far as I can and then drive it forward with as much might as I can manage.

My fist connects with his chin, knocking him off balance again. I push myself up against the fence and slip Pac on my back but when I turn to leave, Spaz is blocking the exit. He's already on his feet and has assumed a fighting stance. Like a wrestler ready to shoot out at his opponent.

He lunges at me. I throw both hands in front of my face and move one foot forward to get a better base so he can't knock me over again. The bottom of the screwdriver handle, still clutched in my fist, pressed against my forehead as I brace for impact.

Just as I step forward, he crashes into me.

I shift all my weight to my front foot.

Spaz's face collides with my hands and I push my body against the force.

But Spaz stops and I don't.

Pac and I fall on top of him.

I feel a gush and a pop as the screwdriver goes through his skull.

His flinching, tweaking body is now limp.

I can't move.

I'm frozen on top of him. Pac is on my back. My hands (still unmoving) are in front of my eyes and the only things separating our faces.

I squeeze my eyes together. Praying this is another bad dream.

A terrible dream.

But as I bring my legs forward, and I find myself sitting on Spaz's lifeless body, with my hand still grasping a screwdriver protruding from his eye socket, I know I won't wake up.

I jerk both my hands back towards my sides; one of them is still firmly gripping the handle.

There's resistance, then another popping sound, before the object is released from his face.

I stand up, straddling him, and stare down.

His head is rolled to the side.

His fingers are bloody from mindlessly clawing at me and Pac.

Blood and puss are oozing from his eye socket.

I kneel down beside him.

What have I done?

I wasn't trying to hurt him.

I was just trying to get away.

I tripped.

It was an accident.

Feelings well up inside my chest.

Feelings I haven't experienced in years.

Guilt.

Regret.

Sadness.

Tears fill my eyes. I slip Pac off and take my phone out.

It's three a.m.

What should I do?

It really was an accident.

A blood test will show that he was baked, drunk, or both. But if I call the police… then I'll have to talk to the police… and that's not exactly flying under the radar.

Then when Paul turns up dead on Monday, why wouldn't they want to question the girl who had just killed someone?

No. No police.

If I would have had a chance to think it through I could have passed it off as a drug overdose but that would be a hard sell now with the hole in his face.

I had no way of anticipating this.

Why? Why Spaz? Why was he out here, away from the security of his group?

They helped keep him in check.
His pill-popping was monitored when he was with Lee.
I don't have time for this now.
I shift my brain from emotions into task mode.
I need to fix this.
Well, I can't fix it.
I need to hide this.
I probably don't have much time until a cleaning crew arrives.
I look down again. His body is twisted in a weird angle.
Blood has pooled around his head.

His body already looks stiff from rigor mortis; or is that just my imagination?

I can't just leave him here.
I look into his unblinking eye. The one that's not gouged out.
It's still wide but no longer bouncing. It's not moving at all.

I let my gaze travel from his face, over the ground, and up the side of the dumpster and I get an idea.

Is that crazy?
Too easy?
I step over Spaz's body and avoid looking at his face.

I lift the lid to the dumpster and stand on my tiptoes to peer inside.

The stench is overpowering. It's dark but I can tell that it's less than halfway full.

I look back down at Spaz's lifeless body.

He's got a few inches and a couple pounds on me but I don't have any choice.

I heave the lid all the way open. It clamors against the fence and I freeze. I hear shuffling and muffled voices. I hold my breath and fight the urge to run away.

To forget Spaz. To forget Paul. And just get out of here.
The footsteps fade. The voices grow quiet.
I size up the situation and decide the best way to approach it.
I can't simply pick him up. He's gangly and dead weight.
Literally.

Elle Iverson

I figure inching him up and in will be the way to go.

As I play through the different options in my head, it occurs to me to check his pockets. He is wearing the same getup as earlier this week. Long t-shirt and baggy pants.

I slip my hands into each of the pockets.

There's a burner phone, small baggies filled with powder (probably heroin) and then my fingers trace over something familiar. My heart races. Really? I pull it out, and sure enough, it is bundled up hundred dollar bills, secured with rubber bands.

Was he buying or selling or both?

Is that why he is here? Did Lee send Spaz as a foot solider to expand his market?

There's no time to think about it. I stuff the phone and cash down along the side of Pac and zip it closed.

I pull Spaz so his back is against the dumpster.

His body hunches forward. His ponytail is falling over his shoulder. A steady stream of blood is pouring from his eye socket. I straddle him and use all my weight to slide his body up the side of the dumpster. He's falling forward. He is heavier than I anticipated.

His arms fling around as I try to hoist him up using the strength of my legs. My arms are shaking under the weight and my quads are burning.

A pungent smell surrounds me. Body odor and cigarettes mixed with blood. It combines with the wafting dumpster tomb awaiting him and I have to swallow to keep from puking.

I finally get him propped up to my height.

I turn around, using my body weight to keep him propped up.

He looks like a rag doll.

I'm completely drained.

Now my legs are shaking too.

I don't know if I'll be able to pull this off.

Maybe I should just walk away.

No, run. Run away. Leave his body here and bolt. By the time the cops find him I'll be long gone.

Avenged Innocence

I start to play through what that would look like. The closest bus terminal, the nearest big town to get lost in… then Paul's face dances through my mind. Followed by sweet little Angela Walker.

I bend down and grab Spaz's knees. I pull as hard as I can, pushing my head and shoulders into his belly. I use all my might, every ounce of strength I have, and I finally hear his head bang against the metal. Then his shoulders slide over the lip of the opening. The rest of his body falls over and then his legs practically flip themselves over. There is an unnerving 'thud' as he hits the bottom.

I drop to my knees and feel around for anything that might have dropped in the struggle.

The screwdriver.

I slip it into the side zipper on Pac.

I wipe the blood onto my jeans.

Nothing else.

At least nothing I can see.

Except the pool of blood.

I take the homeless shirt out of my bag and do my best to wipe up the crimson stain on the ground.

It's still noticeable but there's nothing more I can do but hope people assume it is ketchup and pray for a strong rain soon.

I toss the shirt into the open dumpster, aiming for where I imagine Spaz's face to be. But I can't bring myself to actually look. Then I flip the lid closed and jump when it slams shut and the sound echoes around me.

I swing Pac over my shoulder and walk the long way around the building to the trail. I find a quiet spot, climb to a thick low hanging branch, and finally breathe.

Deep breaths.

I try to let the crisp air cleanse my thoughts, cleanse my mind, quiet my heart.

It's chilly now.

But the weather doesn't bother me.

I can still feel the adrenaline but it's not in the familiar victorious-sense-of-fulfillment-rush I long for.
This has me shaky. Fidgety. Doubting.
Spaz wasn't a bad guy.
He wasn't evil.
He was high.
He wasn't in his right mind.

My heart is swallowed with guilt.
It feels like every beat is pumping tar through my veins and filling my body with dread and regret.
Nothing about this feels good.
Nothing about this feels right.
Nothing about this do I ever want to experience again.

Would a normal person have reacted that way, or am I broken beyond control?

I close my eyes in an effort to calm myself… but every time I do, all I see is Spaz's face… with the gaping hole I put in it.

Have I disillusioned myself into thinking I can control these impulses or are these impulses controlling me?

CHAPTER 34

The sun breaks over the horizon.
The crisp morning air gently blows against my face.
Small woodland creatures scamper around me.
I feel the dew; damp and cool.
One, two, three, four, five, blink.
One, two, three, four, five, blink.
It is now little after seven a.m. The sun is rising and I'm balancing on a tree branch.

It's still quiet out here on the trail. There have been a few early morning joggers but they didn't bother to look around, much less look up.

I've been staring blankly in the direction of the office building for the past four hours.

I still can't believe what happened.

Even though I wish with every fiber of my being that it had been a nightmare, the blood stains on my clothes and the lingering smell of trash and death, portray the truth.

I didn't sleep at all. When my eyes close, even for a second, Spaz's impaled face floods the backs of my lids.

It was my fault really. I hadn't done a thorough job of scoping out the area. I had assumed that since the dumpster was enclosed that it would be safer. I didn't stop to consider that only one exit may make it more dangerous.

One, two, three, four, five, blink.
One, two, three, four, five, blink.
I had tried rationalizing it.
I just can't convince myself that Spaz would have killed me.
He wanted Pac. He had been fixated on it since he first saw it.
Now he is crumpled in a dumpster and I have his money.
I tried reasoning with myself that he had been a drug dealer. He probably dealt to kids and that ruins lives too. But nothing eased my conscious that was singing a chorus on repeat.
"What have you done? I know what you did!"

Between this and Blue Bunny I have a lot of thinking to do and choices to make… but now is not the time or the place. Right now justice for Angela and protecting any future victims from Paul is my priority.

I squeeze my eyes shut and press both palms deep into my sockets, pushing the image of Spaz ever closer to my brain.

The plan.

Focus.

I carefully turn to Pac and take out my extra outfit.

I slowly slip off my black tank top. I spit on the back of it (where there isn't any blood) and use it to wipe my face and arms.

I have no idea if it helps and I really don't care. I pull on my white shirt. Then switch out my jean short for gray yoga pants.

I hop out of the tree, pulling Pac down with me, I head to the fountain. I just need to wait for Paul. Then I can shower. I have to stick with the plan or last night was even more of a waste.

I walk through the parking garage and take out the half dozen cones. I randomly stage them in front of parking spaces on the first and second floors then I hurry out front to the fountain.

I can't see the dumpster from here (it's tucked in on the back of the building) but my gaze drifts in that direction.

I sit on the bench and take out my phone. Timing is critical. That's why I'm here.

Avenged Innocence

There are a few people milling around but no one seems to pay any attention to me as I wait… and try not to think about Spaz.

I run through the timeline again. I just gotta get through this weekend. Then I can have a fresh start.

Cars trickle in the garage.

8:00 passes.

Then 8:05.

And at 8:07, not even ten minutes late, I see the black Maxima turn the corner.

Dang it.

Dang it.

Dang it.

Either he left early or it doesn't take very long to air up a tire.

I wait until I see Paul briskly making his way to the office door and quickly duck inside.

I tuck my phone into Pac and sling it over my shoulder.

The delay portion of the plan will need some tweaking.

Now to investigate the parking situation.

The first level is full.

The cones are still respected but all the other spots are occupied. I walk up to the second level and I notice the Maxima right away. This lot is a little over half full. There are still a quite a few remaining.

Yep. I'm gonna need to make some adjustments.

I'll use the walk back to Regina's to figure out how to buy myself at least another thirty minutes. That'll be a good distraction from Spaz's image flashing through my mind. Now it's not just his blood drenched face that's haunting me but also the first time I met him. How Neeter had introduced us and told me he was a kind boy with funny ways. She had meant his ear flicking. He had shaken my hand and made eye contact but he hadn't said anything. He was always with Lee. And Lee spoke for everyone.

Elle Iverson

I shake my head and try to refocus on Paul.

My mind is a mess. So am I.

I haven't looked in a mirror but I feel awful and I'm sure I look like a wreck.

I'm almost back to Regina's station.

I see a motel promising rooms for $39 a night.

Forty bucks for privacy, a shower, and quiet?

More than worth it.

It's only midmorning but the heavyset, gray-haired clerk doesn't ask any questions when I request a room.

I check in as Susan and pay with cash.

He doesn't even look up when he hands me a key connected to a large plastic card with the number 13 written on it in sharpie.

CHAPTER 35

I lock the door, deadbolt it too, and strip down right there.

I take Pac with me into the bathroom, hoist it on the counter, and turn on the shower.

I have another one of those long, dramatic moments where I stare at myself in the mirror.

Once again, I don't recognize my reflection.

Forget the dark smudges, the sunken holes under my eyes, and the hunched shoulders, my face looks vacant.

I look anguished.

Then Spaz's bouncing gaze covers my own.

I rip my eyes away from the dirty mirror and step under the hot stream of water.

It's scalding hot.

It feels like it's blistering my skin. The boiling pelts of water feel like hot needles hammering away on my flesh.

And I step into it even further. Turning my face into the hot cascade. Welcoming the pain.

There are forces inside my body fighting like I have never experienced.

I have never considered myself a murderer.

Yes, I've killed people. But I don't feel like I've murdered anyone.

Even the first time, at only twelve years old, I had known I had done something wrong, but it was more of a pull between wanting to do it again and knowing I wasn't supposed to.

But I have never felt guilty about it.

I have felt guilt.

I experienced it when I left Mom and the boys.

I have felt guilt for taking daddies away from their children. Even if they were terrible, awful men. I know what it's like to grow up without a father and I feel bad for inflicting that on someone else.

But this... this all-consuming, self-hatred inducing guilt... this is uncharted territory.

For seven years I have known I am a killer.

For seven years I have accepted it as who I am.

But each and every time, every single time, has been justified.

I have eliminated evil.

Avenged the innocent.

Protected the masses.

And, I think on some level, I would consider myself a martyr. I sacrificed being with my family, my happiness, my relationships, for a greater purpose.

For seven years I have been taking lives. But even though I am technically a serial killer, I have never considered myself a murderer.

Until today.

I wash my body. Scrubbing the small hotel soap over every inch of myself until it's fully dissolved into nothing but a lather.

I use the hotel's shampoo and conditioner (all of both) trying to clean the blood and trash smell out of my hair.

I finally turn off the water. Steam is billowing around me and I feel the residual pricks from the scolding water needling me from head to toe.

I wrap one towel around my hair and one towel around my chest and I have an ironic thought about finally having that luxury. All it took was an internal implosion.

I fall, face up, onto the bed.
I stare at the ceiling.
There's so much more to consider now.
My mind is so loud.
Versions of my own voice are talking over each other trying to prioritize.
I try to sort them out.
Try to rationally flip through my choices. But every thought is clouded by the one image that I know will torture me for the rest of my life.
Spaz's eyes.
The one, wide and unmoving.
The other, with my screwdriver protruding from it.

CHAPTER 36

I must have dozed off because I wake up startled and not sure where I am. But it only takes a second and the towel falling off my head, which splays my still-damp hair onto my shoulders, for it to all come flooding back.

The sun is beaming through the blinds.

I stand up slowly. I stretch and let the towel covering my body fall to the floor as I walk to the bathroom.

Pac is still on the counter. I see my murder weapon sticking out of the side pocket.

The events of early this morning have already replayed so much that the sight of the bloody screwdriver doesn't even faze me. I take it out of the pocket and rinse it off. Watching the blood mix with water and create a red pool in the sink. I use my hand to rub off the parts that have dried and are now caked on. Then I use a towel to dry it off, carefully wiping it down like a fragile antique.

I slide it back into the same pouch and notice droplets of blood there too.

Still naked, I slide to the cool bathroom tile, pulling Pac down with me. I wet a rag and methodically clean Pac. Not just the outside but I also take out and examine every item from inside.

My clothes, my Altoids tin, my phone, my blanket, Spaz's phone, and his wad of money.

Avenged Innocence

The shock and anxiety have worn off and now I'm numb.

I look at all my earthly possessions that are scattered out on the bathroom floor and wonder what it all means.

I look at my phone. Still plenty of battery.

I look at the time. Three-fifteen.

More out of habit than actual curiosity, I check PlayRound.

Three new messages.

No surprise there. Chicken, Paul, and Blue Bunny.

Without even opening his envelope, I press down on the chicken until his icon jumps around. The options pop up; reply, unfriend, or report.

I choose to report but don't leave a reason why. Hopefully someone will find him out.

I open Paul's next.

It's a GIF of an Orca breaking the surface of the ocean and the text reads, "Whale Hello There".

I reply back with a laughing emoji as I watch it emotionlessly. Over and over. Allowing my mind to stay blank.

Finally, I click on Blue Bunny's envelope.

"Come out, come out, wherever you are."

I don't even care.

I turn off the phone.

Put back on the white shirt and yoga pants.

I start to rinse the blood out of the clothes. I think about stopping at the coin laundry on the corner, but the thought of ever putting the tank top back on makes my whole body quake.

I use the crumpled up trash bag from Paul's house and shove both sets of clothes in it.

Twisting it around and cramming it into Pac, for now.

There's a thrift store down the block.

Time for a new wardrobe.

I usually wait until after a job is complete before I change anything up.

But this time is different.

So many things will be different.

CHAPTER 37

I had to hustle to make it back to Regina in time.

I checked out of the hotel, picked up a couple new outfits at the thrift store (even splurged on a five pack of new panties at the Dollar Store) and now Regina's warning buzzes in my ears.

"Be here by six o'clock or don't bother coming at all."

I make it to her and the boys just as they are heading down the side of the underpass.

"Was starting to wonder if you were coming back or if you was gonna be out on another all-night adventure." Her tone is quippy but I see a different look in her eyes. Relief? Concern?

It makes my stomach flip. Spaz's gaping hole flashes through my mind and I shake my head to clear the image.

Regina interprets this as a response and probes, "No, you're not back? Or no, it wasn't an adventure?"

I muster up a smile.

"No, no adventure." And I fall in line behind the boys.

The trek to the church, the settling in for the night, the routine in everything is welcome.

But when the boys start reading, and when Regina falls asleep, I'm left staring at the pages of *To Kill A Mockingbird* unable to make sense of any of the words.

Maybe it was the nap today, but more likely, it's the memory from this morning. Either way, I can't sleep.

Avenged Innocence

So instead, I focus on Monday.

I just need to get through this weekend.

I just need to get to Monday.

Any previous excitement I had about the upcoming transaction has been replaced solely with a sense of purpose.

I lay still, staring at the ceiling.

One, two, three, four, five, blink.

One, two, three, four, five, blink.

I hear Regina rustle around.

She stands up and makes her way to the stairs.

I close my eyes and pretend to be sleeping. I do my best to conjure up any image except the one that is so readily available.

"C'mon." She whispers into the darkness. I continue to lay still, waiting to hear one of the boys join her, but nothing.

"Christina, C'mon!" I roll up, grab Pac, and follow her up the stairs. I have no idea what time it is because it's still pitch black.

The silence sits heavily between us.

We walk the whole way to the old-time convenience store without a word.

We enter and are greeted by a different clerk than last time, but he also recognizes Regina.

She smiles and they engage in chitchat as we fill up our coffees, grab the donuts, and pay.

She remains silent until we come to the spot on the curb where we stopped before. She sits and motions for me to do the same.

The concrete is still cool; I take a sip of the hot coffee and let it warm my body.

She starts off with the matter-of-fact tone again.

There's no small talk, no segue; she simply picks up the conversation where we had left it two days ago.

"Tyrone has been a blessing to our family ever since." (I picture Regina waiting in the hospital. The tiny baby hooked up to all those wires. His little body fighting to survive.)

"Him and Michael have grown up like brothers. He knows his mama left him with me because she was sick but that's all. Mike and I worked hard to give these boys everything. And we did. They was in sports, boy scouts, any activity they wanted.

Michael's business was going good. We wasn't makin millions, but it was puttin food on the table and it kept us living comfortably. I worked part time at a chiropractor's office filling out paperwork and answering phones. I enjoyed it and it gave us extra money each month.

I did everything I knew to do to be a good mama and a good wife. Then, two years ago, my perfect world crashed. It was October 27th. I remember every detail. I came home from buying candy for trick or treaters. The boys was at school. I set the groceries on the counter and about jumped outta my skin when I turned and seen Mike on the floor, curled up in a little ball, rockin back and forth. This giant of a man actin like an abused little child."

She paused to take a sip of her coffee. I was waiting for tears or anger but she continued in the same monotone voice.

"He told me he was in trouble. He got in bad with some bad people. I just stared at him. Waiting for the punch line. He said he was sorry. He didn't know how it got this bad, but now they were after him. He owed big and didn't know how he was going to pay it back.

Christina, I had so many questions runnin through my mind at one time.

Who? Who did he owe? How much? How in the blazes had he been gamblin without me having so much as an inkling? What did he mean they were *after him*?

But none of them seemed as important as the one question I asked. 'What are we gonna do?' He looked up at me with those big beautiful brown eyes that had tears brimming over, spilling onto his cheeks and his face changed from despair to…. Well, it looked like a lightbulb went off. Like you seen with them cartoon characters. His whole face was different.

Avenged Innocence

I was so mad at him I coulda killed him with a spatula right then, just beat him to death in our kitchen for being such an idiot. But I knew that wouldn't solve anything. So we planned. We had savings accounts for both boys to go to college, not a lot in 'um, but there was some. We cashed those out. We had a little nest egg for retirement, cashed that out. Mike already had loans out in his name against his business but I took out a personal loan. We sold my car, for way under value, but got paid in cash. We scraped together every penny we could. It wasn't enough, I still don't know exactly how much he owed… but he was the love of my life so we did everything we could in the short time we had before his deadline. Then he had his meeting with 'the bad people'. He took everything we had pulled together with him in a suitcase and kissed me on the way out the door. That was the last time I saw him."

I search her face for grief or sadness but she doesn't portray any emotion. I don't know what to say so I hang my head and whisper, "Oh Regina, I'm so sorry."

She finally turns to me, her eyes burning with fire, "Sorry for what?"

She is visibly angry. That wasn't the reaction I had expected.

"Uhh… I'm… I'm sorry for your loss. Sorry they killed him."

"No one killed him, Child. He ran. He took every penny we had and the sorry son of Satan ran away.

About an hour after he kissed me and told me that he loved me, there was a knock on our door.

Two men askin for Mike. I said he was at a meeting and they just looked at each other, then they both looked back at me.

That's when I knew.

I don't know how the thought hadn't crossed my mind before, but I had two realizations in that instant.

Number one: Mike had taken the cowards way out and run. Leavin me alone with our two boys.

Number two: People like this don't just accept that the person who owes them money bailed. They expect their payment. I had no doubt they'd chase down my numbskull husband, take what money he hadn't spent, and then kill him. I also knew his debt needed to be paid. And I was the only one to do it.

As I thought, a couple days later the brutes showed up again. This time they had a very generous offer; sees how I was left in such a bad way, they would only expect me to pay a fraction of what Mike owed. They explained that it's bad for business if an entire debt is forgiven just because the shmuck disappears.

Can't have that word getting around. So if I paid twenty thousand dollars within two weeks, well then, they wouldn't kill my boys. Wasn't that thoughtful?" She sneered into her coffee.

"I was workin twenty hours a week, makin ten bucks an hour. It would have taken me a lifetime to pay back that kind of money.

I didn't sleep for three days. I racked my brain tryin to think of a way out of that mess. I kept circling back to one option.

I had to sell the house. My mama and daddy's house. A lady at our church was a realtor. I called her the next morning. We listed it quick.

Oversized Thing One and Oversized Thing Two showed up a few nights later to check in and make sure the boys and I hadn't been as fool-headed as my idiot husband. I told them what I was going to do. Told them I was hurrying and asked if there was any way I could get a little more time.

They came back the next day with the answer.

Absolutely. I could absolutely have more time. But each additional week would add ten thousand dollars to my total.

Christina, I have never known stress like that. Not before and not since. I called the realtor. She came over and I told her as much as she needed to know. Bottom line; I needed the house sold… and cash in hand… yesterday.

Her company ended up buying the house. I don't know the specifics of how it works but what I do know is that I got a check for $75,000 the next day. The house had been listed for $125,000. But I didn't care.

Avenged Innocence

I went straight to the bank. I paid back the twenty thousand dollar loan I had taken out. Paid the thirty thousand dollar debt Michael had against his business and the twenty grand to the thugs that had started the whole mess.

If you're doin the math, that leaves about five grand. But that went into a savings account to cover taxes and penalties for selling the house and takin out of our retirement early. I don't know how much it'll end up bein' but Michael is long gone. The last thing I need is to be thrown in jail for tax fraud or some nonsense.

Yes, we were debt free. But we were also homeless and word had gotten around as to why. The chiropractor I worked for didn't want his business affiliated with anything remotely related to those thugs, I didn't blame him, but I couldn't find another job."

Another pause for coffee.

When she speaks again her tone is lighter.

"This is where our story starts to turn around. Word had also gotten to Tyrone's daddy. His name is Malik. I had never met him before. According to Malik, my sister didn't tell him about the baby until Tyrone was over a year old. By then Tyrone was settled in with us and doing well. But it was a wakeup call for Malik. He changed his life around and became a pastor for a small church outside of town. He didn't have much money but when he heard about our unfortunate circumstances, he offered to let us stay in the basement of his church building til we could get on our feet.

I accepted.

I've left that money untouched 'cept what already went to the IRS, and I've been adding to it whenever I can. By the time school starts next month the boys and I will have a permanent place to live. When I walk away from beggin', I'm walkin away for good. Starting today I'm looking for an apartment and I'm fillin out applications. I never wanted my boys to beg. I never wanted this life for them. But good can come out of any situation. The boys have always been good kids, but now, now they are grateful. Life got a little perspective. They gotta whole lotta respect for their Mama and they seen exactly the type of man they don't wanna be. Those boys are what got me through that and now we're so close to starting over."

She pauses and takes a deep breath.

"I like you Christina, I do. I want to help you. But, honey, if you're up to no good I need to know and I need you to not bring it around my babies. We've been through a lot and I'd even say we're better for it... But we've been through enough."

I tear my eyes away from her gaze and stare at the ground.

Well that explains their church situation and why the boys are so exceptional.

I kick my shoe into the concrete and notice a dark smudge on the side of the sole. Blood.

"I'm lost." I didn't even have a chance to think about it before the words fell out of my mouth. "I thought I knew my purpose. I thought I had my life sorta figured out. Now everything is different. Confusing."

"What's different? What happened?" Her tone is soft. "Christina, I really do want to help you."

I believe her. She had just shared her deepest truths with me and I think she actually cares.

The confessions bubble up to my lips. My heart seems to open. Feelings of trust and the anticipation of the freedom that truth brings overwhelm me.

I want to tell her everything. I want to have one person to talk to, one person who can help me. But before words can express the confessions of my heart, my mind quickly closes my mouth. I feel gates slam shut and the quench the light that was filling me internally.

I can't.

I never will.

I know she would help.

It's possible she may even understand.

Avenged Innocence

But I can't put that on her. What I want for her and the boys is for them to live their happily ever after. I would do anything in my power to help them get that.

My secrets are my burden to bear.

No one else's.

So instead of unloading my past, my passions, and my new burden of guilt, I simply say "Thank you."

This time I'm the one to stand up, with so much left unsaid, and walk back to the church in silence.

CHAPTER 38

The rest of Saturday and all of Sunday were uneventful. I finished the book, thanked Tyrone, and he put it back in his library. I treated everyone to a nice Sunday dinner at a buffet. I was legitimately impressed by how much the boys ate. We definitely got our money's worth. I tried to soak up every ounce of energy, integrity, and ambition that I could from the three of them.

Even though they were a part of my life for such a short time, I know they've made a lasting impact. I will never forget Regina's story. Not just the series of events, but how she has let them mold her into a better person and how she hasn't let them skew her world view. She is still kind, generous, and optimistic.

I know she would help me. It's possible she may even understand. But I can't put that on her. What I want for her and the boys is for them to live their happily ever after. I will do anything in my power to help make that happen.

That's why, right now, I'm leaving Spaz's cash (along with a note expressing those same sentiments) in my nook at the bottom of the stairs before I sneak out.

I didn't sleep a wink last night. I haven't slept much all weekend but now it's four a.m. and I'm wide awake.

I quietly open the door and I'm greeted by a cool breeze. The sky is clear and dark.

Here we go.

Avenged Innocence

Today is the day.

That familiar rush is back.

My heart is beating fast and my mind is sharp and alert.

I don't know how to correlate the sickness I feel about what I did to Spaz with the adrenaline rush I have for what I'm about to do to Paul. But it's a welcome change of pace.

I am excited.

I am also nervous because I had to build in an additional step to ensure Paul is detained long enough for me to get in position and for the traffic in the parking garage to quiet down. It's an elevated risk since I haven't actually tested it yet, but I don't have time. Plus, I know I'm leaving town after I'm done.

Like, immediately after. Before Paul's body is even cold I plan on being on a bus headed west.

I draw in a deep breath and bob my head along to the song playing in it, one of my dad's favorites, 'Don't Stop Believin'.

I make it to Aspen Views by four-thirty.

The house is completely dark. I see a light on down the road but no activity. I slide the screwdriver out of Pac and a shiver runs through me.

Spaz's face flashes before my eyes.

Focus, Christina. I mentally push the image away and unscrew the valve cap. The tire wheezes as the air releases. My eyes dart around, scanning for any movement.

I'm so close to the finish line.

I watch the tire slowly deflate. I flatten it a little more than I had on Thursday night. I need Paul to stop to air it up and I need him to stop somewhere close. Satisfied with my work, I re-pocket the screwdriver, screw the cap back on, and sling Pac over my shoulders with one more glance at the house.

Still dark.

Perfect.

I walk quickly out of the subdivision, almost jogging, until I get to the highway.

Step one done.

Now comes one of the toughest parts of the whole plan.

Waiting.

I'll have to wait two hours.

The gas station shines like a beacon a little ways down the road. I slow down to what could be described as a shuffle and start checking things off in my mind.

After the waiting, then things will happen quickly. Two hours of downtime followed by one hour of fast-paced exact precision.

I run through the whole thing one more time.

I configure and reconfigure the timing.

It will have to be just right.

The highway is mostly deserted.

A few semi-trucks blow past but I doubt they're giving me a second look.

I take a few steps into the ditch; the grass is damp with dew so I sit on the gravel shoulders. I move the screwdriver from the outside pocket to one inside.

I'll get rid of it as soon as today is over. I don't want it around as a constant reminder.

I take out my phone and check the time.

It's not even five-thirty yet.

I stare at the screen. The phone is a touchscreen but it's an old one. It was one of the first things I did after I got here. I got Christina a phone plan.

I see people glued to their phones all day long. Staring at the screen, looking for it to fill some need. Entertained for hours (sometimes days) by a small device barely bigger than their hands. I'm not judging, I just never had that luxury. I had a cell phone when I was fourteen but my mom strictly monitored it and I was forbidden from social media until I was sixteen.

Since I was tragically murdered at the ripe young age of fifteen, Aurora never had social media.

Now I have social media but Christina doesn't have any friends.

Avenged Innocence

Social media (or a cell phone in general) is much less addicting when seeing other people only makes you feel lonelier. I've been tempted to look up my mom or my brothers. Tempted, but I never have. I don't want to put myself through that.

It's hard enough to snap back to reality after the few times I allow my mind to wander and reminisce. To actually see them (or worse, to feel some connection to where they are now) would be excruciating.

It's painful to play through memories of happy times so I don't do that often.

What I never think about is my last night as Aurora.

The night I staged my own death.

Chapter 39

I was fifteen.

I told mom I was staying overnight at Tara's.

I had been using Pac as my school backpack all year so it wasn't suspicious when I left that morning with it stuffed full.

That whole day felt like an eternity and I talked myself out of my plan more times than I can count. But at the end of school, I knew that it was what was best for my family. So right after the last bell, I hid in the woods behind a nearby park.

Just before dark, I took half of my blankie (that I had ripped down the middle) and threw it in the river just upstream from a dam where I knew it would get caught.

I also took off the shirt I had worn to school and dropped it near the water.

I ran my fingers through my hair and let a few strands fall. Then I retraced my steps back to the school. That's where I sprayed myself down with two different scent-masking sprays and placed scent-removal pouches in my pockets. I had found a whole row human scent deterrent in the hunting section of the outdoors store. Of the three options I selected, I hoped at least one would throw off the police dogs.

I slipped on my black witch's wig from my Halloween costume and wore Pac backwards underneath my large homeless t-shirt. I wanted to look overweight or pregnant; not look like Aurora wearing a wig and carrying Pac.

Avenged Innocence

I walked the five miles to the bus station.

Then I was on the midnight train to Georgia.

Well, the midnight bus to Dallas, but you get the idea.

As far as I know (from what I could piece together from news broadcasts) they had issued an Amber alert for me. They used the school picture with my pigtails and bright smile... it was a slight resemblance to the scraggly look I adapted as soon as I stepped on that southbound bus.

Aurora was plastered all over the news for a couple days. But after the evidence was found by the river, and the trail went cold, the news cycle shifted.

There had been a few blurbs about the connection between the previous murders around The Cities but it wasn't the serial killer manhunt I had suspected.

Regardless, the plan had worked well enough.

I'm hoping tonight's plan will go as smoothly.

I slide the phone in the front pocket of Pac. I need to keep it accessible. My stomach grumbles, reminding me that I've been too excited to eat. I take a granola bar from Pac and try to savor it as the minutes creep by. My anxiety builds with each passing second.

Finally, it's time to walk to the gas station. I grab my new oversized t-shirt and slip it on over my new green tank top. I acquired quite the wardrobe at the fancy thrift store. These, along with the skinny jeans and faded ball cap I picked up, should be the perfect blend-in ensemble.

The door chimes when I enter.

It's a different clerk than the last time but he still looks at me skeptically as he offers the standard, "Good morning."

There are a few more people in here today.

I loiter around the store, pretending to decide which of the stale-looking, unappetizing, pastries I'd like to try. I settle on a chocolate long john. Then I wander over to the coffee counter, trying not to be obvious as I stare out the window, watching for the Maxima.

I fix my coffee and feel the anxiety building again.
What if he doesn't stop here?
What if he doesn't notice the tire?
What if he noticed but decided to take Gretchen's car instead of stopping to fix his?

I walk to the counter, unintentionally ignoring the clerk's small talk. I'm too involved with my own inner dialog to pay any attention to him. I can't afford to stay any longer.

It's now or never with Paul.
The plans have been put in motion.
There is no second chance.

If I vanish today, I could still run from Blue Bunny and tip off the police to what Paul is up to… but what would they find?

Just as I'm about to admit defeat, just as I'm accepting that this plan won't play out, I see the black Maxima slowly turning into the lot.

I gather up my coffee and doughnut and take out my phone. I press a few buttons, activating step three, and smile.

I slightly pop the lid off the coffee up and wait for Paul to crouch down by the tire.

Go time.

While I pretend to be texting, I take a take a few bites of the sweet but stale snacks and begin executing step two.

I hold my phone in one hand and place the donut on top of the jarred coffee cup in the other. Then I back out of the door, being careful not to look where I'm going.

I step off the sidewalk and head toward the gas pumps.

When I get a few feet from Paul, I let myself trip and fall.

Hard.

To his credit, he turns and tries to catch me (I guess he's not completely heartless, just evil) and he ends up with my coffee all over his shirt and pants.

"I'm so sorry! Ohmygosh! I'm so sorry!" I try to force tears but they won't come so I dial up the drama instead. I had let my phone drop to the concrete. It landed next to Paul. He hands it to me as he stands up and examines his drenched outfit.

The screen is cracked.

I had assumed that would happen and I was fine with it. An added element of flair.

I wouldn't be using it after today anyway.

"Dang it! Dang it! Dang it!" I even stomp my foot for good measure. I'm trying to span this out for five minutes or so.

"I'm so sorry." I say again.

Paul no longer looks concerned about me.

"Are you okay?" He snaps rather than asks.

I take a second to inspect my scraped arms and legs and mumble, "Yeah, I think so."

But he has already moved on. He's screwing the cap back onto the air valve and winding up the air hose.

"Damn it! I don't have time for this!" He yells at no one in particular. Then gets back in his car and revs the engine as he backs out. I watch the blinker expectantly.

C'mon. C'mon. C'mon.

When the right blinker turns on and he accelerates back towards his house I am able to breathe again.

Step two done.

I watch the Maxima drive out of sight and I shift my focus to looking for the red jeep. I had Ubered for a ride as soon as I had spotted the Maxima. I was happy when Lexi's face popped up on my screen. I'm only a few miles from the McDonald's where she picked me up at before, and it's roughly the same time of day.

A welcomed coincidence.

I took it as a sign of good luck and apparently it had been.

The spilled coffee had worked nicely to buy me an extra twenty or twenty-five minutes with Paul and now the timing of the red jeep pulling in was serendipitous.

CHAPTER 40

"Well there's a familiar face!" Lexi exclaims as she pulls to a stop, bringing the back passenger door right in front of me. "You're a backseat girl, right?"

I remind myself that it doesn't matter that she remembers me, I'll be gone after today.

"You betcha!" I say as I jump in. I hope it doesn't sound as phony as it felt. But then with genuine interest I add, "Hey, you promised to fill me in on the rest of the story about your boyfriend who had a wife and another girlfriend."

I can't think about my plan anymore. The distraction will be nice.

"Mmmhmmm. That's a good one. First, I wanna make sure we're goin in the right direction. You're headed back to the same place? More shoppin?"

"Yep, same place. Just finishing up. I was scoping out some things before. Now it's time to commit…"

"Gotcha. Ok well, here's the skinny." A smile and wink in the rearview mirror and she's off. "I'd been dating Dreamboat for six months. He was sophisticated, had some big time job as an ad executive, and traveled a lot but was always real good to call or text first thing in the morning and at night. Whenever he wasn't traveling he'd take me on these movie-worthy dates. I had so many dear-diary moments with him that I could've published a romance novel.

Anywho, he proposes. I'm elated. He tells me to plan the wedding of my dreams. Says he wants it to be my fairytale come true. Well honey, I'm deliriously happy and I'm babbling to anyone who will listen about my Prince Charming.

Fast forward to wedding dress shopping… my doting groom-to-be had thoughtfully provided me with a list of stores to check out but my best friend insisted we go into the city… to one of those swanky boutiques that serves champagne while you shop.

There I was, blabbering about how incredibly lucky I was, how over the moon excited we were, how perfect he was, every little detail about the proposal… and then I show the sweet little sales girl the picture we took right after he asked me to be his wife; him grinning ear to ear, me flashing my rock of a diamond at the camera.

As soon as she saw the picture she got this look on her face.

You know how sometimes you just know? I just knew. I had no idea how twisted and tangled the mess would be, but the instant her face fell from a smile, my heart dropped to my stomach."

For the first time Lexi's own smile falters. She glances in the rearview mirror and I see the pain on her face that she works so hard to keep at bay.

With a deep breath she keeps going, "To give the sales girl credit, she didn't come right out with it. I pestered her until she finally caved. She said she couldn't be sure, but my fiancé looked an awful lot like another girls' fiancé she had helped last week.

At first, I was so devastated I wanted to die. I left the shop right away and my friend drove me home where I bawled for two days straight.

Then I started second guessing. What if she had been wrong? What if it wasn't him? What if I let myself get all worked up for no reason. Well, then I felt stupid. So I did what any sane, rational, smart, and sophisticated woman would do."

This warranted another wink in the mirror.

"I followed him. I had never been to his office or his house. I felt like a cop on a stakeout, slinking down in the front seat of my friends' car. Staying a couple car lengths behind him. At first, he met with other business-lookin guys." She furrows her brow as she turned into the mall parking lot. "Long story short, I ended up following him to a house then meeting the woman he lived with. We teamed up and found out we weren't the only ones. It turns out he used the weddings, extravagant lifestyles, and home remodels to clean money for a not-very-prestigious organization. Then he'd let the marriages dissolve and let his wife file for divorce while he walked away free as bird and still filthy rich thanks to an ironclad pre-nup."

"Charming." That's all I can come up with to say as we pull to a complete stop. I have to get out. I have stuff to do.

But I hate to bail after that story.

Sensing my hesitation Lexi resumes her upbeat cheerleader tone, "Listen sweetie, it's fine. He wasn't the first money-hungry, self-involved, polygamist to break my heart and he probably won't be the last."

I hand her a hundred dollars.

"Thanks for the ride. Good luck." Without looking back, I grab Pac and hoof it to the parking garage. It's already filling up. I slide my cracked phone out of my pocket and check the time. I should have twenty more minutes. Thirty if traffic got bad. I open the door under the stairs and breathe a sigh of relief at the sight of the cones that are still there. I had been worried that, since I'd been placing them out sporadically the past few days, someone might get sick of putting them away and remove them or lock the storage room door. But all the worry was for naught because there they stood. In all the glorious orangeness. I place four in the remaining open spots on the first level and haul the rest upstairs to the second level. There are still a few cars coming in. I walk with confidence and purpose and no one questions what I'm doing. I get a little anxious when there are still open spots after the last of the cones are in place; but there's nothing I can do about it now.

I head up to the third level of the parking garage and begin the final stint of waiting.

The three cars from before are already in position.

Good.

I slip Pac off and prop it along the side of the walled-off stairwell. I take out my stun gun and put away my phone.

I scoot Pac around so it's out of sight and walk to the opposite side of the big black Hummer and crouch down.

I can see the entrance. My heart beat accelerates. I visualize coming up behind Paul, startling him, stunning him, but as he falls backwards, his face morphs into Spaz's.

My body quakes. I try to concentrate on my breathing and regulating my heartbeat.

I conjure up the image of little Angela Walker.

That works.

The little girls' face floods my mind. I feel my body still, my heartrate slows, and my breathing deepens.

I take out the stun gun, slide the button to the on position…

And I wait.

The black nose of a car slowly rounds the corner.

My legs tense, readying.

Chapter 41

I see the emblem on the hood and queasiness fills my gut as I realize it's a BMW.

The driver comes into view and it's a pretty blonde wearing oversized sunglasses.

No. No. No. No. No. No.

She pulls to a stop a few spots down from the Hummer. I make sure my body is lined up with the tire so she can't see me and I hold my breath.

I hear her door open and one high heel clips the concrete.

Then nothing.

Maybe she's gathering her purse.

Maybe she's fixing her makeup.

Maybe she saw me and she's calling security.

I'm praying for her to hurry up and for Paul to slow down. My ears are straining to hear any indication that she's leaving while also listening for the sounds of an approaching car.

I hadn't realized I was holding my breath until her other shoe clicked down, I hear the car door slam shut, she quickly clip-clops toward the stairwell, and my lungs let out a giant gust of air.

I let myself enjoy a few more calming breaths then I hear another car approaching.

This is it.

Avenged Innocence

My eyes focus on the entrance. Right in the middle, praying for the Nissan logo.

I see the black body as it accelerates into the near-empty lot. The emblem and driver both come into view. My eyes register the hood logo and the deceptively handsome face immediately.

Paul swings the car into an empty spot close to the entrance. His door opens as he kills the engine.

I stay low and duck-walk to the back of the Hummer and around the side. Ideally he would have parked where BMW lady did because then I would have the advantage of sneaking in behind him.

Now I have to hurry, I only have the element of surprise.

I come out from around the back of the Hummer (between it and the Beamer) and stand up straight. I walk quickly to Paul who has just shut the door and is rounding the front of the car.

I yell, "Excuse me!"

He is so focused on getting to work that he hadn't noticed me. Startled by the sound of my voice, he turns around and a fleeting look of recognition passes over his face as I press the stun gun into his groin. I hold the trigger.

His body convulses. Tightening from head to toe. His eyes bulge out. His neck snaps back and then forward.

I'm anticipating all of this, of course. I have my head down protectively to avoid his thrashing limbs. After a few seconds he cries out in pain. A delay from the shock.

He falls to his knees, cradling his precious area.

Watching him intently, I kick his shoulder and he topples backwards, not moving his hands. Denying me anymore access to his now swelling genitals.

Confusion joins the anguish in his eyes.

Without losing any momentum from the kick I use the force of my whole body to pounce on top of him.

My legs are posted out, securing his. My hands are rigid in the upside down field goal position.

I don't have much time. He's strong. My quick reflexes and lack of tazered-ness are my only advantages.

Thanks to his protective gesture of covering his manhood (which has both his arms at his sides) I can easily put my knees on his elbows. My feet press into his thighs and angle with more pressure directly onto his windpipe. I put all my weight onto my hands.

I listen to him gurgle and cough.

He's gasping and choking. I feel his throat crushing.

I feel the power. I feel the control.

I feel the size of him. I feel the muscled, domineering, psychopath, writhing beneath my legs.

I watch his face turn red, deepening shades of red.

The adrenaline courses through me and warms my body.

My limbs are working together in the almost-natural process; arms and legs securely locked in place, fingers rigid, eyes trained on the light in this monster.

I wait for it.

I let the rainbow start to flood over me.

I feel his legs (weaker but still flinching) trying to throw me off.

His hands, pulling on my arms.

His eyes. They've already stopped frantically searching.

The fear is slowly leaving as the realization that this is the end sinks in.

The only element missing is the high.

The euphoric feeling.

The release.

This is the pinnacle for me; when the evil light goes out. When one more predator realizes they'll never get to hunt again.

Cleansing the world of one of the baddest of the bad guys.

His eyes roll back and his body goes limp beneath me.

The light is out. The evil is extinguished.

But the feeling never comes.

Avenged Innocence

There's actually more of an emptiness as Spaz's face briefly crosses over Paul's.

If I reel back now there's a chance his body will react, it might try to breathe or fight.

I close my eyes and push the image away and lean into his throat with every ounce of energy I have left.

This confirms it.

Paul will be my last kill.

He has to be.

My purpose is muddled now. I need to start over, to reevaluate.

I thought I had been given a gift. I thought I had a special calling, but now my abilities are tainted.

Now that I'm lacking the affirmation (worse than that, I'm doubting) I can't take any more lives; even ones deserving of worse than death.

I stare into Paul's vacant eyes. My resolve to never kill again is as strong as the desire *to* kill had been when I started my mission four years ago.

I'll have to find a new way to bring justice.

I'll have to find something that ignites my passions and fills me with satisfaction, other than extinguishing evil.

I count to thirty and when there's still no movement, I roll back on my haunches and slip the discarded stun-gun into my back pocket before standing up. I step over the body and look around for anything else that may have fallen in the struggle.

I stoop down to grab Paul's wallet when a slow-clapping sound from behind me causes me to jump.

CHAPTER 42

I spin around. My entire body is tensed up with fear.

Standing in front of the stairwell is a lanky, clean-cut, TV-dad looking guy.

Danny Tanner of the twenty-first century.

I recognize him but I can't remember from where.

Panic fills my gut.

He smiles as he continues the solo-slow-clap and takes a few steps towards me.

"I thought that was you at the gas station. Pretty ingenious. Let me guess; you were the reason his tire was low in the first place, amiright?"

He smiles at his own cleverness, revealing white, perfectly straight teeth.

My internal alarms are going haywire and my stomach is doing flip-flops.

"Who are you?" I sound more confident than I feel.

"Don't you recognize me? Maybe if I had on my sunglasses and headphones…"

My heart stops.

"You're Blue Bunny."

"Is that what you nicknamed me? After a stuffed animal or ice cream? Not very original for a girl as clever as you. I had hoped for better." He sneers.

Avenged Innocence

"What do you want? What are you doing? How did you find me?" My heart and mind are both racing.

"Slow down, Christina. Can I call you Christina? You can stop the wheels turning right now and listen." With that, he reaches behind his back and brings out a gun from his waistband.

A gun.

Coward.

"What we're gonna do first is get the hell outta here. I'm not some idiot who will stand here and monologue to give you time to come up with some hair-brained escape idea. C'mon. Nice and easy." He gestures for me to walk in front of him.

Pac is still tucked out of sight but when Paul's body is found, I'm sure the cops will confiscate it.

I can't have that.

"You're just gonna leave him here?" I gesture to the body. "This place is covered with cameras. When they find him, that's the first thing they'll check."

I see his brow furrow slightly.

I think he's either trying to figure out if I'm lying or what his next move should be.

A car door slams shut on the street below and we both jump.

"Hurry up!" He keeps the gun pointed at me but motions towards Paul.

"Get his keys." I do.

"Pop the trunk." I do.

"Get him in there." I stare at the normal-looking guy pointing a gun at me. Then over at Paul's body. Then back to Blue Bunny.

"How?" Now I am stalling.

It's been at least ten minutes since Paul arrived. If someone shows up and sees Blue Bunny with a gun trained on me, and a dead body between us, no one will believe I had anything to do with it.

Just a poor teenage girl in the wrong place at the wrong time.

"I'm not messing around, Girlie. Do it."

I grab Paul under the arms. With my head next to his, I dead lift his upper body to the trunk.

My mind flashes to Spaz. Hoisting his body into the dumpster. I shake my head to clear the image.

Not the time, Christina. Not the time.

I use my knees to help lift.

I manage to get his top half up and in.

I lean against the trunk, which is now warming from the sun, and take a few deep breaths.

"Hustle. I'm not playing around." Blue Bunny (the name is eerily fitting; disarming and innocent) waves his gun for effect.

I squat down and heave Paul's legs inside the trunk too.

His body rolls so he is facing the front of the car. I have to push his feet up, moving his knees toward his chest, to close the truck. Paul's body is in the fetal position.

I look at Blue Bunny and he nods.

"Now we walk."

CHAPTER 43

With the gun still trained on me, he shoos me to the door.

I hold my breath as we pass Pac. I don't have any idea what's going to happen or what I'm going to do. I don't want to grab Pac now. But I don't want the police to find it.

We walk into the stairwell and he's close behind me.

The gun is digging into my shoulder as I walk down the steps.

"Make a move or a sound and I'll shoot you."

A pretty cliché line but I think he means it.

I don't want to die. I like living. But that threat alone isn't enough for me to subject myself to whatever he has in mind. I would rather be dead than forced to do his bidding.

But if I die and they find my body then they will run my DNA. Then they'll tell my mama.

She'll know I ran away. She'll have so many questions that she'll never know the answer to… I can't do that to her.

I won't.

"We're going to the first level. Mine is the white Taurus. I moved one of your cones. That was a nice touch."

We walk into the empty first level and I see his car right away.

We get over to it and I move to get in the backseat.

But he blocks me.

"No, No. You drive."

"I can't. I've literally never driven a car before."

He looks annoyed but concedes.

"Fine, but get in the front. You're not gonna use any of your ninja moves on me from behind."

I slide in and close the door.

Is this really happening?

I am usually so careful. So cautious.

The thing with Spaz has been weighing so heavily on my mind that I must've slipped.

Ok, no reason to rehash that now

Now is the time for planning.

Ideas flash through my head.

I feel the comforting edge of the stun gun digging into my hipbone. I pull my legs up in front of me and hug them with my arms. I'm thankful for my oversized shirt that hangs low enough to hide the fact that I'm sitting slightly tilted.

"Don't give me that innocent, scared-girl bit. Na-uh. I know what you are."

I start fiddling with my shoe laces.

"I don't know what you're talking about."

"PlayRound." He says flatly.

Before I can even think, my head shoots up and I meet his gaze. Our eyes lock.

I finally break away and look out the front windshield.

We're driving through a small suburb that I've never been through before.

"No comment?" He asks sarcastically.

"I don't know what you're talking about..."

"Mmmhmmm. That's how you're gonna play it? Ok, Ms. Smarty Pants. I work for a company that creates on-line apps. My job isn't very glamorous. I write code and fix glitches. All low level except for one application. It's my favorite. When I saw it on the launch board, let's just say it really piqued my interest, if you know what I mean. It combined two of my favorite things; technology and little kids"

He looks over at me waiting for a reaction.

I don't give him the satisfaction of one so he keeps going.

"See, up to that point I'd pretty much had to do things the old-fashioned way. Watch schools, playgrounds, and parks. But when the bright and bubbly Laura Hangroove created this app as a 'safe space' for kids to make friends, I was intrigued. See, a lot of apps have safeguards for parents. There are a lot of known evils on social media that are closely monitored. But our little project was a much smaller scale. More along the lines of the 'Buddy Bench' that some schools are implementing. Well, it didn't take me long playing around in the back office of the program to see that I wasn't the only one with less than noble intentions."

Again, a sideways glance checking for a reaction.

Again, I remain stone-faced.

Again, he continues.

"Laura would be happy to know that a vast majority of users really are young kids. Their search history and online time includes silly YouTube videos and Lego searches. But there were a few others whose browsing histories mirrored mine. Or it would if I was dumb enough to leave a browsing history…"

"So how did you find me?"

"It was luck really. I had been snooping on Elliot Neelbrook. Does that name not ring a bell? You probably knew him as Hannah."

I knew Elliot Neelbrook. I had killed him after setting up a meeting with Hannah.

"Anyway, one day Elliot has no more activity. His last message was to a kitten named Kacey. I didn't think much of it until a few months later when I stumbled on Nathan Smith who also, suddenly, didn't have any more activity after talking to a pink teddy bear. Just to satisfy my curiosity, I checked the Mac address where those accounts originated. Guess what I found?"

He raises his voice in mock surprise and puts a hand over his heart. "They were one and the same. So then I looked up past uses from that same address and, lo and behold, five avatars

Elle Iverson

linked to five inactive accounts. Curious, hmm? So then I checked out who you were now, read up on those messages, and tracked you down. It was quite simple."

I thought I had been so clever by only using my phone and always having the location turned off...

"I almost had you at the playground but you're a really great actress. When I saw you bolt I had already passed you over because you seemed so disinterested. I had moved on. After you left, I walked to the girls you had used.. I mean, befriended, and found out your name. The rest was just for fun."

That's where I had seen him! The park. He was the guy by the tree without any kids. The one I thought could have been Paul.

Ironic.

I finally ask a question, "Ok, so why catch me? Why not tell the others what I was up to? Why not just warn the other creeps? Why catch me?"

He looks at me while caressing the gun in his lap.

"Well, see, normally I tend to fancy girls much younger than you. Six to eight years old is really my preference. Still innocent. Still so sweet. But you intrigued me. Brains are a turn on too.

Most of the other guys on there are idiots. That's why I don't warn them. It's also why I try to keep tabs on them, so they don't get discovered and blow my cover. I'm smart about it. See, you don't want to take a high fluent white girl. They draw too much attention. You gotta be selective. That's why, even with all these apps, well, I still keep my job at the Y on the weekends. Those poor little girls don't have a daddy and their mama is too busy doing her thing. All they want is a little lovin... and that's what I give 'um. A little lovin."

A twisted smile curls his thin lips around his pearly whites.

I can't look at him anymore.

I put my feet down and stare out my window.

CHAPTER 44

We pull up to the backside of a small, but nice looking, strip mall in a populated area.

I had expected a trailer in the middle of nowhere.

Or an abandoned house with a cellar.

No, this is in a populated commercial development. Across the street there is a monstrous gym, a doctor's office, and an auto body shop.

When I look back over at Blue Bunny he is smiling from ear to ear. Obviously proud of himself.

"Here's the kicker. We're minutes away from my office so my alibi is readily available." With a wink and a click of his tongue he points the gun at me and nods his head toward an unmarked door. Then, as if just remembering it, he adds; "Oh yeah, and don't forget, try anything and I'll kill you. Let's go."

He slips the weapon back into his waistband and we both step out of the car.

There are people going in and out of the other buildings and even out of the other doors of the mall. There are cars driving by and people on the sidewalks.

And no one notices.

No one sees the frantic pleading in my eyes as we walk the few feet from the car to the back door.

Elle Iverson

His gun isn't easily accessible. I could run. Just start sprinting. But what if he opens fire? What if he misses and shoots someone else? What if he doesn't miss and shoots me? Even if it doesn't kill me, they'll be an ambulance and police officers... and what if the police link me to Spaz's murder. What if they link me to Spaz's murder AND find out who I am... or who I was.

No. No getaway attempt.

We walk in to an empty space. It looks like a room waiting to be set up for a one-man business operation. Like a small insurance space or maybe a massage parlor.

It's only one room and I see the front door, along with the wall of windows, is tinted so no one can see in.

There are two other doors inside. Both are open.

One is a bathroom.

The other is an office.

Everything looks normal enough.

He takes the gun out of his waistband and waves it toward the office. I walk into the small room. There are no windows in here. It smells stale.

He sets his phone and keys down on the desk.

He holds the gun on me but doesn't bother to tie me up. I am guessing that intimidation is usually enough for him.

The only decoration is a bulletin board hanging on the wall. Tacked to it are friendship bracelets. The colorful ones made of yarn or string. Tara, Chelly, Grace, and I used to make them for each other all the time.

He shuts and locks the door, then walks over to the bracelets. As if transfixed by them. He runs his fingers over them one by one as he talks. A smirk playing across his face.

"Don't worry. This is sound proof. It's not usually a problem getting the girls this far. A promise of candy and some quality time and they're quite compliant.

Do you want to know the best part?

I never kill them after the first time.

And I don't even keep them here.

No, I like to play puppet master for a couple months. Young girls are very moldable, and with the right motivation, they can be very cooperative.

Just tellin' them that I'll slit their mama's throat or drown their baby brother if they say anything and they are quite obliging. I'll have my fun for a few months. Then after she's ruined, when that sparkle is completely gone from her eyes, then I'll kill her. But first, first I let her make me something to remember her by."

He looks from me to the bracelets then back to me with a maniacal smile. He's looking again for a reaction from me and this time I can't help it.

Disgust and terror are written all over my face.

He likes it.

He slowly walks over to me, holding the gun in front of him like a shield as he bends down by my face.

His hot breath sticks to my skin.

"Take a deep breath. Can you smell that? The coconut still hangs in the air from little Maria. Her mama was Latina and her daddy was black. She was beautiful. She had that thick black curly hair and she used to rub oil on it… there would be some on her hands; it rubbed off onto her bracelet. I can still smell it in here. She was one of my favorites. I kept her around for almost three months. But that's not the record. The record is four months… that title belongs to Aaliyah."

His eyes are dancing. He is enjoying this. He likes bragging about his conquests.

He's not trying to impress me. He's trying to disgust me.

He's trying to get a reaction.

Keeping the gun between us, he reaches out his other hand and tucks a lock of hair behind my ear. Then he uses the back of his hand to caress my cheek and he continues talking, but now it's in a whispered, intimate tone. How I imagine sweet nothings would be exchanged over pillow talk.

"I know all their names. I think about them all the - …"

Elle Iverson

I knock my forehead into his nose as hard as I can. When he stumbles back, his gun drops to the floor. I grab my stun gun from my back pocket and I am standing over top of him within seconds.

I put the stun gun under his chin and hold it on until the count of ten.

How's that for a reaction?

His body shakes and convulses.

His eyes roll back. I shove the stun gun in my back pocket as I bend over him.

Now is my chance. I could drop down, assume the field goal stance, and end him.

End his pathetic, miserable, awful life.

I could look at the bracelets hanging on the wall as I make sure he never hurts anyone again.

But I can't.

Instead of strangling him, my arms roll him over, grab his hands, and use my shoe strings to tie his wrists together.

I hadn't been sure what I would use them for, but while he was monologue-ing in the car, I had unlaced both my shoes and slipped the laces in my pocket.

Now I kick off my loose shoes and grab his phone.

He's starting to regain his bearings back and get to his knees.

He's yelling at me, "Stupid girl. Stupid, stupid, girl."

He makes it to his feet and stands between me and the door.

I grab his gun from the floor.

I didn't want to do this.

But I have to.

I aim and fire.

He drops to the ground.

I leap over him and run out of the office.

I dial 911 on his phone and throw it in the corner of the big room as I run out the back door.

Avenged Innocence

I burst through and when the sun hits me I feel like an escaping POW. Even though I had been held captive less than an hour, I still feel violated. And now liberated.

I take off at a sprint around the corner.

I have to get away from here.

Far away.

CHAPTER 45

I don't have my phone and I don't have my Altoid money but I do have Paul's wallet.

I slowdown from my sprint and take the wallet from my back pocket. It has a few hundred dollars in cash, a few credit cards, and his ID.

This will work.

I shove the cash in my pockets and drop the wallet in a garbage can as I run across the street and scan up and down in both directions.

Back to the right is definitely busier. I see stop lights and what could be a bus station about a mile away.

My feet pound against the concrete as I run in that direction. My chest is heaving and my legs feel like Jello. I am unable to fully catch my breath. It's probably close to eleven a.m. and there's light traffic, enough for people to look at me funny running in stocking feet. I don't care. I gotta get outta Dodge.

I make it to the bus stop without collapsing. A miracle in itself. I do my best to reteach my body how to inhale then exhale, because my lungs are trying to do both at the same time.

I grasp my sides as I try to get my bearings and study the map.

Ok, I see the 'You are Here' and I see the business complex. It looks like there are only a few stops in between.

Avenged Innocence

I warily look behind me for any indication of Blue Bunny but there isn't any.

It wasn't easy to choose to shoot him in the leg instead of his face or stomach, but knowing that the police will respond to the 911 call (and I'm counting on them to discover the monster he is) eases my conscience.

I fold myself onto the waiting bench opposite an overweight gentleman who looks at me and smiles. He nods and gives me a slight wave with his sausage-like fingers. I give him a polite smile back then focus on my feet. My socks are black from the asphalt. I feel my heartbeat in my soles from the pounding on the asphalt.

I need to figure out what to do.

Everything feels so surreal.

What just happened?

Was I really kidnapped?

I killed someone then got kidnapped from the scene of the crime? How does that even happen?

And Blue Bunny, I never did get his real name, he is sick.

Sick and twisted, but I couldn't kill him. I had let him live.

If I can just get back to the parking garage then I can get Pac and resume my plan from where I was interrupted by this little life-threatening detour.

Unless I don't.

Unless I just leave now.

A bus pulls to a stop out front.

No time for second guessing. I hurry to the self-service kiosk and pay cash for a one-way ticket.

One decision down.

I'll figure out the rest later.

I take my ticket and impatiently stand at the end of the line. I shuffle along with the five other people who were waiting under the canopy, and we climb on board.

I find an empty row towards the back and slide in by the window. I fix my eyes on the door. I highly doubt he's going to come after me in such an obvious place, but you never know.

I strain my ears to listen for police sirens. They should be at the strip mall by now.

They should trace the 911 call from his phone and find him.

But I don't hear anything.

His eyes. His eyes were evil. I've seen my share of hate-filled and scary eyes but his were some of the worst.

Yet, I didn't kill him.

I don't know how I feel about that.

My stomach hurts when I think about the terrible, awful things he's done… but killing is no longer my role.

Something changed when Spaz died.

Something is different.

I crave the feeling.

I crave the rainbow.

But now when I think about killing, I feel the negative connotation that it has always carried with the rest of society.

The bus stops and a few passengers exit (including the friendly guy from the bench) and a few new faces get on.
No Blue Bunny.
I slowly rock back and forth in my seat, taking in the last views of the city.

I will miss Dallas.

I will miss Regina and the boys.

I will miss Christina.

I have grown to love her.

I was free. Lonely at times, but free.

I had become solid in my purpose. I had found resolve and fulfillment.

Now… Now I'll be starting all over.

Again.

EPILOGUE

I'm sitting at my oversized desk that takes up half of my small office, mindlessly passing my phone from one hand to the other as I listen to the woman across from me explain why she thinks her husband is having an affair.

I've in been in San Diego for two years now.

Another new life.

As soon as I got off the bus from Dallas I went to work on starting over.

Completely over.

No Pac.

No Blankie.

No Phone.

Ultimately I didn't want to take the chance of going to the office complex and risk a police presence.

I literally only had the clothes on my back and the little bit of cash from Paul.

After a few weeks of begging, I had enough money to find someone to make me someone new.

And just like that, Reigh was born. You remember Ray, right? The trucker who helped me get to my meeting with Paul. The one who changed his route for his family. I liked him. And Reigh, as a girl's name is cute, quippy, and kinda catchy.

After a couple months of scrounging, panhandling, and a convincing sob story to the landlord about my parents being killed and losing everything in a fire, I secured this teeny tiny office space that doubles as my apartment. It's nothing fancy but it is a huge step up from the dumpster and treetops I was residing in before.

I couldn't shake the urge to hunt bad guys but now I do it under the guise of a private investigator.

The certificate listing my qualifications (which my ID guy also made) is hanging on the wall behind me.

I watch the pretty brunette across from me dab her eyes as she tells me about her husband's late nights at the office, the mysterious phone calls, and his lack of attraction to her. I nod my head and make a few notes on the pad of papers sitting on my desk.

I've convinced myself that this is helpful too. I'm giving wives peace of mind, or exposing cheating husbands.

Yes, I'm still doing good… even though it doesn't give me the purpose or the high that other activities did.

In an effort to chase the rainbow, if you will, I've taken up surfing. It's not the same but there is definitely an adrenaline rush that compares.

As for purpose… I still bait perverts online. I still track. But I forward my leads to the police department.

Mainly to a detective I met when one of my first cheating husbands got caught with his seventeen-year-old student. Aaron was lead on the case.

We didn't exactly work together (he pretty much interrogated me) but he is open to the leads I give him. Once in a while he'll let me know how they turn out. It tends to be over dinner.

Aaron is attractive. He is very attractive. But nothing has happened. That part, that part is still confusing to me.

I've controlled the urges and impulses.

I've psychoanalyzed myself through the addiction, but I'm nervous that intimacy will trigger something.

I've let my mind wander about the handsome detective joining me for an early morning surf… catching the waves… laying on the sand… one of the things I love about living here are the beaches.

Eventually I'd like to have an office that overlooks the ocean but for now I settle for this riveting view of a city street. I'm tucked between a pawn shop and a tattoo parlor, across the street there is a small bakery that makes amazing cream cheese pastries. My gaze drifts longingly to the window and I can almost taste the flaky crust and warm filling; but my attention is drawn to the bench just outside the bakery, on the opposite side of the street facing my front window.

A balloon drifts in front of the six dollar per dozen sign.

But it's what the balloon is attached to that takes my breath away.

I excuse myself from the leaking customer and walk to the door. I push it open and cross the street, without bothering to look for cars.

I run to the bench and my heart stops.

Chills run up my spine.

On the bench, wearing headphones and dark sunglasses, with the balloon string tied around its wrist so it appears to be waving, is a large stuffed blue bunny.

I spin around, scanning the whole street, but I don't see him.

I notice a small note pinned to the front of the stuffed animal, gently fluttering in the breeze.

My hands are shaking as I pull the piece of paper closer to my face, though I don't need to because I can clearly see the two short sentences written in black sharpie.

I STILL know who you are.
I STILL know what you did.

Here we go again.

Acknowledgements

My Husband: Thanks for letting me test out violent methods, act through attack scenes, and for giving me so many ideas. Oh yeah, and for your unwavering support and stuff…

My Kids: For thinking it's cool that your mom writes thriller stories and for telling everyone we know that I like killing people.

My Momma: For passing down the love of all things murder and for always being the first to read every word I publish.

My Dad: Thanks for not disowning me and for supporting me, even in things you don't agree with… like spending countless hours thinking out homicidal scenarios.

My Brothers: My protectors. My fans. My friends. I love you.

My Five: My small circle of friends who let me talk out the crazy (in my books and all aspects of my life). You are some of the best people I've ever met and a main source of my material. I am infinitely blessed by each of you.

Christina: For being the first character to speak to me so clearly. For needing your story told and for walking me through such a whirlwind of emotions to produce, what I think is, a fantastic book. You are my star.

Made in the USA
Columbia, SC
12 April 2019